She Slipped Off Her Sunglasses, And The World Skipped A Beat.

The unforgiving heat, lack of road signs and the problems waiting for him in Dallas slid away.

Clear blue eyes peered up at him out of a heart-shaped face and a riot of cinnamon-colored hair curled against porcelain cheeks. Not a glimmer of makeup graced her skin, unusual enough in itself to earn a second glance. The sun bathed her in its glow, a perfect key light. She was fresh, innocent and breathtakingly beautiful. Like a living sunflower. He wanted to film her.

She eyed him. *"Problema con el coche, señor?"*

Kris closed his mouth and cleared his throat. "I'm Greek, not Hispanic."

"Wow. Yes, you are, with a sexy accent and everything. Say something else," she commanded, and circled a finger. The blue of her eyes turned sultry. "Tell me your life is meaningless without me, and you'd give a thousand fortunes to make me yours."

Somehow his mouth was open again. "Seriously?"

She laughed, a pure sound that trilled through his abdomen. A potent addition to the come-hither she radiated like perfume.

"Only if you mean it," sh

Dear Reader,

I first started writing this book many years ago, but it stalled because I couldn't find the core story I wanted to tell. I loved the characters and couldn't forget them. All I knew about them was that they started in one place but ended up in another. It was only with a lot of work on my storytelling skills, plus a good bit of distance and time, that I realized *that* was the core story: the journey. I scrapped almost all of the original manuscript—yes, it was *hard*—and started over. What emerged is what you hold in your hands today. It's the story of two people in completely different places, emotionally and physically. Destiny intervenes and their individual journeys merge. I love how it turned out, but I love even more how it parallels my own journey of becoming a published author.

This book is my version of *Cinderella,* with a couple of nods to *Pretty Woman.* The story lacked only a magic wand, and I am eternally grateful for the one my editor, Stacy Boyd, waved over it. I hope you enjoy reading the result! VJ and Kris have lived in my head for a long time, and I'm so excited to finally share their happily-ever-after with you. I'd love to hear your thoughts. Visit me online at www.katcantrell.com.

Kat Cantrell

KAT CANTRELL

THE THINGS SHE SAYS

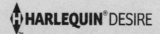

Recycling programs
for this product may
not exist in your area.

ISBN-13: 978-0-373-73231-9

THE THINGS SHE SAYS

Copyright © 2013 by Katrina Williams

This edition published by arrangement with Harlequin Books S.A.

For questions and comments about the quality of this book, please contact us at CustomerService@Harlequin.com.

Printed in U.S.A.

Books by Kat Cantrell

Harlequin Desire

Marriage with Benefits #2212
The Things She Says #2218

Other titles by this author available in ebook format.

KAT CANTRELL

read her first Harlequin novel in third grade and has been scribbling in notebooks since she learned to spell. What else would she write but romance? She majored in literature, officially with the intent to teach, but somehow ended up buried in middle management at Corporate América, until she became a stay-at-home mom and full-time writer.

Kat, her husband and their two boys live in north Texas. When she's not writing about characters on the journey to happily-ever-after, she can be found at a soccer game, watching the TV show *Friends* or listening to '80s music.

Kat was the 2011 Harlequin So You Think You Can Write winner and a 2012 RWA Golden Heart finalist for best unpublished series contemporary manuscript.

To Cynthia Justlin, the sister of my heart.
You wouldn't let me give up on this book
and I'll never forget it. Thank you for all the years of
cheerleading, support, gentle critiques, encouragement
and friendship. I'm so happy we're sharing this journey.

One

The only thing worse than being lost was being lost in Texas. In August.

Kris Demetrious slumped against the back end of his borrowed, screaming-yellow Ferrari, peeled the shirt from his damp chest and flipped his phone vertical. With the new orientation, the lines on the map still didn't resemble the concrete stretching out under the tires. Lesson for the day—internet maps only worked if they were accurate.

The Ferrari was no help with its MP3 player docking station but no internal GPS. Italian automotive engineers either never got lost or didn't care where they were going.

Mountains enclosed the landscape in every direction, but unlike L.A., none of them were marked. No mansions, no Hollywood sign and no clues to use to correct his wrong turn.

He never got lost on the set. Give him a controlled, detached position behind the camera, and if the scene refused to come together, starting over was as simple as yelling, "Cut."

So what had possessed him to drive to Dallas instead of fly?

A stall tactic, that's what.

Dying in the desert wasn't on his to-do list, but avoiding his destination was. If he could find food and water, he'd prefer to stay lost. Because as soon as he got to Dallas, he'd have to announce his engagement to America's Sweetheart Kyla Monroe. And even though he'd agreed to her scheme, he'd rather trash six weeks' worth of dailies than go through with it.

He pocketed the phone as bright afternoon sunshine beat down, a thousand times hotter than it might have been if he'd been wearing a color other than black. Heat shimmered across the road, blurring the horizon.

Just then, churning dust billowed up, the only movement he'd seen in at least fifteen minutes. A dull orange pickup truck, coated with rust, drove through the center of the dirt cloud and pulled off the highway, braking on the shoulder behind the Ferrari. Sand whipped against Kris in a gritty whirlwind. He swept his hair out of his face and went to greet his rescuer.

Really, once he ran out of gas, he could have been stuck here for days, fending off the vultures with nothing more than a smartphone and polarized sunglasses. He'd already spun the car around twice to head in the opposite direction and now he'd lost his bearings. The truck driver's timing was awesome and, with any luck, he would be able to give Kris directions to the main highway.

After a beat, the truck's door creaked open and light hit the faded logo stenciled on the orange paint. Big Bobby's Garage Serving You Since 1956. Dusty, cracked boots appeared below the opened door and *whoomped* to the ground. Out of the settling dust, a small figure emerged. A girl. Barely of driving age and, odds are, not Big Bobby.

"Car problems, chief?" she drawled as she approached. Her Texas accent was as thick as the dust, but her voice rolled out musically. She slipped off her sunglasses, and the world skipped a beat. The unforgiving heat, lack of road signs and the problems waiting for him in Dallas slid away.

Clear blue eyes peered up at him out of a heart-shaped face and a riot of cinnamon-colored hair curled against porcelain cheeks. Not a glimmer of makeup graced her skin, unusual enough in itself to earn a second glance. The sun bathed her in its glow, a perfect key light. He wouldn't even need a fill light to get the shot. She was fresh, innocent and breathtakingly beautiful. Like a living sunflower. He wanted to film her.

She eyed him. *"Problema con el coche, señor?"*

Kris closed his mouth and cleared his throat. "I'm Greek, not Hispanic."

What a snappy response, and not entirely true—he'd renounced his Greek citizenship at sixteen and considered himself American through and through. How had such a small person shut down his brain in less than thirty seconds?

"Wow. Yes, you are, with a sexy accent and everything. Say something else," she commanded and circled a finger. The blue of her eyes turned sultry. "Tell me your life is meaningless without me, and you'd give a thousand fortunes to make me yours."

Somehow his mouth was open again. "Seriously?"

She laughed, a pure sound that trilled through his abdomen. A potent addition to the come-hither she radiated like perfume.

"Only if you mean it," she said.

There was too much confidence in the set of her shoulders for her to be a teenager. Mid-twenties at least. But then, how worldly could a girl from Nowhere, Texas, be? Especially given her obvious fondness for romantic melodrama and her distinct lack of self-preservation. For all she knew, he might be the next Charles Manson instead of the next Scorsese.

With a grin, she jerked her chin. "I'll cut you a break, Tonto. You can talk about whatever you want. We don't see many fancy foreigners in these parts, but I'd be happy to check you out. I mean check *it* out." She shook her head and shut her eyes for a blink. "The car. I'll look at it for you. Might be an easy fix."

The car? She must work as a mechanic at Big Bobby's. Intriguing. Most women needed help finding the gas tank.

"It's not broken down. I'm just lost," he clarified while his imagination galloped back to the idea of her checking him out, doctor-style, with lots of hands-on analysis. Clawing hunger stabbed through him, as unexpected as it was powerful.

Maybe he should remember his own age, which wasn't seventeen. Women propositioned him all the time, but with the subtlety of a 747 at takeoff, which he'd never liked and never thought twice about refusing. He had little use for any sort of liaison unless it was fictional and part of his vision for bringing a story to the screen.

This woman had managed to pull him out from behind the lens with a couple of sentences. It was unnerving.

"Lost, huh?" Her gaze raked over him from top to toe. "Lucky for me I found you, then. Does that put you in my debt?"

Everything spilled out of her mouth with veiled insinuation. When combined with her guileless demeanor and fresh face, the punch was forceful. "Well, you haven't done anything for me. Yet."

Slim eyebrows jerked up in fascination. "What would you like for me to do?"

He leaned in close enough to catch a whiff of her hair. Coconut and grease, a combination he would have sworn wasn't the least bit arousing before now. Same for the big T-shirt with the cracked Texas Christian University Horned Frogs emblem and cheap jeans. On her, haute couture.

He crooked a finger and she crowded into his space, which felt mysteriously natural, as if they'd often conspired together.

"Right now, there's only one thing I'd like for you to do," he said.

His gaze slid to her lips and what had started as a flirtatious game veered into dangerous territory as he anticipated kissing this nameless desert mirage, sliding against those pink lips, delving into her hot mouth. Her laugh pulsing against his skin.

Kissing strangers was so not his style, and he was suddenly sad it wasn't.

"Yeah? What would you like me to do?" She wet her lips with the very tip of her tongue, heating his blood all the way to his toes.

"Tell me where I am."

Her musical laugh poleaxed him again. "Little Crooked Creek Road. Also known as the middle of nowhere."

"There's a creek somewhere in all this sand?" Water—wet, cool and perfect for skinny dipping.

No. No naked strangers. What was wrong with him?

"Nah." Her nose wrinkled, screwing up her features in a charming way. "It dried up in the 1800s. We lack the imagination to rename the road."

"So tell me, since you're local. Is it always this hot?" Truthfully, he'd long stopped caring about his sticky, damp clothes, but the urge to keep her talking wouldn't go away.

"No, not at all. Usually it's hotter. That's why we don't wear all black when it's a hundred and ten," she said, scrutinizing him with a gaze as sizzling as the concrete. "Though I like it on you. What brought you so far off the beaten path, anyway?"

"I wish the story was more interesting than a wrong turn. But it's not." He grinned and tried to be sorry he'd veered from the interstate but couldn't conjure up a shred of regret. Surprisingly, being in the middle of this scene wasn't so bad. "I left El Paso pretty sure I was headed in the right direction, but I haven't seen a sign for Dallas in a long time."

"Yeah. You're lost. This road winds south to the Rio Grande. It's really not grand or even much of a *rio*. Can't recommend it as a sightseeing venture, so I'd head back to Van Horn and take the 10 east."

"Van Horn. I vaguely remember passing through it."

"Not much to remember. I was just in town, and it hasn't changed since the last time I came in March. Speaking of which, I need to get a move on. The part I picked up isn't going to magically install itself in Gus's truck." She sighed and stuck a thumb over her shoulder. "Van Horn's that way. Good luck and watch for state troopers. They live to pull over fast cars.

"Or," she continued brightly, "you can go thataway and take your first right. That'll put you on the road to the center of Little Crooked Creek and the best fried chicken in the county."

He wasn't nearly sated enough on the harmony of her voice. Or the charming way she rambled about nothing but piqued his interest anyway. Real life loomed on the horizon, and even if it took him a month to arrive to Dallas, he'd still be unhappy with the creative financing deal for *Visions of Black*. Kyla would still be Kyla—unfaithful, selfish and artificial—and he'd have to expend way too much energy not caring.

But, he reminded himself again, it was worth it. If he wanted to make *Visions,* he had to generate plenty of free publicity with an engagement to his beloved-by-the-masses, Oscar-winning ex-girlfriend. A fake engagement.

"Fried chicken is my favorite." And he was starving. What could a couple of hours hurt? After all, he'd driven on purpose so it would take as long as possible to reach Dallas. "What's Little Crooked Creek?"

"The poorest excuse for a small town you'll ever have the misfortune to visit in your life," she said with a wry twist of her lips. "It's where I live."

The Greek god was following her. VJ sneaked another glance in the rearview mirror. Yup. The *muy amarilla* Ferrari kept pace with Daddy's truck. God had dropped off a fantasy on the side of the road in a place where nothing had happened for a millennium and he was *following her*.

Giddy. That was the word for the jumpy crickets in her stomach. She'd been waiting a long time for a knight in shining armor of her very own and never in a million years would she have expected to find one until she escaped Little Crooked Creek forever, amen. Yet, here he was, six feet of gorgeousness in the flesh and following her to Pearl's. Shiver and a half.

She pulled into a parking place at the diner and curled her lip at the white flatbed in the next spot. Great. Lenny and Billy were here. Must be later than she thought. Her brothers never crawled out of bed until three o'clock and usually only then because she booted them awake, threatening them with no breakfast if they didn't move their lazy butts.

Hopefully they weren't on their second cup of coffee yet and wouldn't notice the stranger strolling through Pearl's. The last thing she wanted was to expose her precious knight to the two stupidest good ol' boys in West Texas.

The Ferrari rolled into the spot on the other side of Daddy's truck, and the Greek god flowed out of it like warm molasses. He was the most delicious thing in four states, and he was all hers. For now. She wasn't deluded enough to think such an urbane, sophisticated specimen of a man would stick around, but it was no crime to bask in his gloriousness until he flowed back out of her life. Sigh. She grabbed her backpack and met him on the sidewalk.

Pearl's was almost empty. Her stranger was as out of place as a June bug in January, and it only took fourteen seconds for all eight pairs of eyes in the place to focus on them as she led him past the scarred tables to the booth in the shadow of the kitchen—the one everyone understood was reserved for couples who wanted privacy. She plopped onto the bench, opting to take the side sloppily repaired with silver duct tape and giving him the mostly okay seat.

He slid onto the opposite bench and folded his pianist's fingers into a neat crosshatch pattern right over the heart carved into the Formica tabletop, with the initials LT & SR in the center. Laurie and Steve had been married nearly twenty years now, a small-town staple completely in contrast to this man, who doubtlessly frequented chic sushi bars and classy night-clubs.

What had she been thinking when she invited him here?

"Interesting place," he said.

Dilapidated, dark and smelling of rancid grease maybe, but *interesting* wasn't a descriptor of Pearl's. "Best cooking you'll find for miles. And the only cooking."

He laughed and she scoured her memory for something else funny to say so she could hear that deep rumble again. Then she abandoned that idea as he pierced her with those incred-ible melty-brown eyes. She settled for drinking him in. He was finely sculpted, as if carved from marble and deemed so per-fect that his creator had breathed life into his statue and set it free to live amongst mere mortals.

"My name's Kris." He held out a hand and raised his eye-brows expectantly. "From Los Angeles."

Surreptitiously, she wiped the grime and sweat off her palm and clasped his smooth hand. Energy leaped between them, shocking her with a funny little zap.

"Sorry, static electricity. It's dry this time of year." She folded her hand into her lap, cradling it with the other. Was it too melodramatic to vow never to wash it again? "I'm VJ. From nowhere. And I'll keep being from nowhere if I don't get to work. I'm saving every dime to get out of here."

She jumped up, hating to desert him, but it was almost four o'clock.

"You're leaving me?" Kris cocked his head and a silky strand of his shoulder-length hair fell into his face. She knot-ted her fingers behind her back so she couldn't indulge the urge to sweep it from his cheekbone. Touching the artwork was a no-no, even when it wasn't behind glass.

"Not a chance," she said. "I have to put my uniform on, then I'll take your order."

He glanced at the other customers, who weren't ashamed

to be caught in open inspection of the foreigner in their midst. "You work here?"

His accent was amazing. The words were English, a language she'd used her entire life, but every syllable sounded exotic and special. It was the difference between Detroit and Italy—both produced cars, but the end result had little in common other than tires and a steering wheel.

And it was way past time to stop rubbernecking. "Uh, yeah. Five days a week."

Her brothers lumbered off their stools at the counter. Out of the corner of her eye, she watched them hulk over to the booth.

"Who's the pansy?" Lenny sneered. VJ butted him in the chest with her shoulder until he glanced down.

"Back off," she demanded. "He's just passing through and no threat to you. Let him be."

Lenny flicked her out of the way as if she weighed no more than a feather.

Before she'd fully regained her balance, Kris exploded from the booth and descended by her side, staring down Lenny and Billy without flinching. Okay, so maybe he didn't actually need defending. Her heart tumbled to her knees as he angled his body, shielding her, unconcerned about the five hundred pounds of Lewis boys glaring at him. Nobody in Little Crooked Creek stood up to even one of her brothers, let alone two. He really *was* heroic.

"Kristian Demetrious. You are?" His face had gone hard and imperious—warrior-like, about to charge into battle, sword drawn and shield high. As if she needed another push to imagine him as her fantasy knight, come to rescue her from Small Town, USA.

Then his full name registered.

She blinked rapidly, but the image in black didn't waver. Kristian Demetrious was standing in the middle of Pearl's. No one would believe it. Pictures. Should she take pictures? He looked totally different in person. Gak, he probably thought she was a complete hick for not recognizing him. She had to call Pamela Sue this very minute.

Right after she made sure Lenny and Billy weren't about to wipe the floor with Kyla Monroe's fiancé.

"These are two of my brothers. They like to play rough but they're mostly harmless," she said to Kris. "I apologize. They don't get day passes from the mental institution very often."

With a hard push to each of her brothers' chests, she said, "Go sit down and drink another cup of coffee on me. Cool off. Mr. Demetrious isn't here to pick a fight with you."

And just by saying his name, Kris turned into someone remote and inaccessible. A stone rolled onto her chest. He was Kyla Monroe's fiancé. Of course he was. Men like him were always with women like Kyla—gorgeous, elegant and famous, with a shelf full of awards. Well, she'd known her Greek knight was out of her league but she hadn't known he was *that* far out. Actually, she'd thought maybe he was flirting with her a little—but he couldn't have been. She'd misinterpreted his innocent comments, twisting them into something out of a romance novel.

Lenny and Billy skulked away, shooting spiteful glances over their shoulders, and hefted themselves onto their stools, where they eyed Kris over their earthenware mugs. Cretins.

"I'm afraid you've discovered my secret superpower. I'm a moron magnet." She met Kris's eyes. "Thanks. For standing up for me."

How inadequate. But what could she say to encapsulate the magic of that defense from someone like Kristian Demetrious? Small to him, huge to her.

He shrugged and flipped hair out of his face, looking uncomfortable. "One of my hot buttons. So, it's Mr. Demetrious now?" He slid onto the bench. All the hard edges melted and he smiled wryly when she opted to remain standing. She couldn't sit at the same table like they were even remotely in the same stratosphere. "I'm not a fan of formality. I introduced myself as Kris for a reason. Can't we go back to being friendly?"

His smile was so infectious, so stunning as it spread over his straight, white teeth, she returned it before catching herself. "No, we can't. My mama raised me to be respectful."

"I liked it better when you were being disrespectful." He sighed. "Obviously you know who I am. I'm going to guess it's because of Kyla and not because you've seen my films."

"Sorry. I read *People* magazine, of course, but we're lucky to get a couple of wide releases at the theater in Van Horn. For this corner of the world, the films you direct are entirely too… what's the word?" She snapped her fingers. *"Cosmopolitan."*

"Obscure," he said at the same time, and something passed across his features. Determination. Passion. "That's going to change. Soon."

"I have to clock in." And put some distance between them before she asked him how and when. What his work was like, his plans. His dreams. She could listen to him talk all night. Sophisticated conversation, the likes of which she'd never had the opportunity to participate in.

She turned to go. His fingers grazed her arm, and tightened with a luscious pressure, holding her in place. What a thrill it would be to have that golden hand—both hands—wandering all over, undressing, caressing—and enough of that, now.

"Change fast. I'm starving," he said, his eyes went liquid and a brow quirked up. Before realizing he was taken, that was the kind of comment she would have misread, mistaking his smoldering expression as invitation.

"You're the boss. I'll be back in a jiffy."

She edged away, terrified if she shifted her eyes, he'd disappear.

So what if he did? He belonged to Kyla Monroe, the blonde goddess of the screen.

Her stomach flipped. They were from different worlds. He

was only here by an accident of navigation, not some divine plan to make all her wildest dreams come true.

Kristian Demetrious was another woman's man who'd landed in the middle of Little Crooked Creek for a heartbeat and then would be gone.

Two

Kris leaned against the hard booth and watched his desert mirage do a dozen mundane things. Punching her time card in the antiquated machine mounted to the wall of the open kitchen. Making a phone call at the honest-to-God pay phone nestled between the upright video game and the bathrooms.

She moved with vibrancy, like the progression of a blooming flower caught in time-release photographs. Suddenly bursting with color and life. Magnificence where a moment before had been nothing special. Where was his camera when he really needed it? Anything that visceral should be captured through the lens for all posterity.

No. Not for anyone else. Only for his private-viewing pleasure. A selfish secret celebrating artistry instead of capitalism. Maybe that was the key to unlocking the yet-to-be-conceptualized theme for *Visions of Black,* a frustration he'd carried for weeks.

The light in this dive was sallow and dim. All wrong. He'd position her outside, with the late-afternoon sun in her face and mountains rising behind in an uncultivated backdrop. Maybe an interview, so he could capture that mellifluous drawl and the unapologetic raw honesty. With VJ, everything was on the surface, in her eyes and on her tongue, and he was greedy for transparency after drowning in Hollywood games.

He'd left his condo in L.A. before dawn this morning, intending to drive straight through to Dallas, where he'd meet up with Kyla to start the engagement publicity and get rolling on preproduction work for *Visions*.

But one more Kyla-free night now felt less like a reprieve and more like a requirement.

He just wanted to make films, not deal with financing and publicity and endless Hollywood bureaucracy. *Visions of Black* was the right vehicle to propel his career to the next level, with the perfect blend of accessible characters, high-stakes drama and a tension-filled plot. Audiences would love Kyla in the starring role, and her charisma on the screen was unparalleled. She was a necessary part of the package, first and foremost because executive producer Jack Abrams insisted, but Kris couldn't disagree with the dual benefit of box-office draw and high-profile PR.

The need to commit this story to film flared strongly enough that he was willing to deal with his ex and any other obstacles thrown in his path.

Tomorrow.

VJ skirted the tables and rejoined him, smiling expectantly. "Fried chicken?"

"Absolutely." Nobody in L.A. ate fried chicken and the hearty smell of it had been teasing him since he walked through the door. "And a beer."

"Excellent choice. Except you're in the middle of the Bible Belt. Coke instead?" she offered.

"You don't serve alcohol?" A glance around the diner answered that question. Every glass was filled with deep brown liquid. Five bucks said it was outrageously sweet tea.

"Sorry. I'm afraid it's dry as a bone here." She leaned in close and waggled her eyebrows. "We're all good Baptists. Except behind closed doors, you know."

He knew. Where he came from, everyone was Greek Orthodox except behind closed doors. Different label, same hypocrisy. "Coke is fine."

"I'll have it right out for you, sir."

He almost groaned. "You can stop with the sir nonsense. Come right back. Keep me company," he said.

Keep the locals at bay. A convenient excuse, but a poor one. He liked VJ, and he'd have to leave soon enough. Was it terrible to record as much of her as possible through the camera in his head until then?

"I can't. I'm working."

"Doing what?" He waved at the dining room. "This place is practically empty."

Her probing gaze roamed over his face, as if searching for something, and the pursuit was so affecting, he felt oddly compelled to give it to her, no matter what it was.

"Okay," she said. "But only for a few minutes."

She glided through the haphazard maze of tables and bent over her order pad, then handed it to the middle-aged woman in the kitchen. Pearl, if he had to guess.

The brutish brothers, clearly adopted, continued to shoot malevolent grimaces over their shoulders, but hadn't left their stools again.

Only a couple of things were guaranteed to rile Kris's temper—challenging his artistic vision and picking on someone weaker. Otherwise, he stayed out of it. Drama belonged on the screen, not in real life.

A slender young woman with a wholesome face whirled into the diner and flew to VJ's side. Amused, he crossed his arms as they whispered furiously to each other while shooting him fascinated glances under their lashes. Benign gawking, especially by someone who intrigued him as much as VJ did, was sort of flattering. After a couple of minutes, the other woman flounced to the bar, her sidelong gaping at him so exaggerated she almost tripped over her sandals.

"Friend of yours?" he asked as VJ approached his table.

VJ was giving him a wide berth, something he normally appreciated, but not today and not with her. There'd been an easiness between them earlier, as if they'd been friends for a long time, before she got uptight about his connection to Kyla. Friends were hard to come by in Hollywood, especially for someone who cultivated a reputation for being driven and moody. He lost little sleep over it. Different story with VJ, who made the idea of being so disconnected unappealing.

"Yeah, practically since birth. That's Pamela Sue. She's only here to ogle you."

He laughed. "I'm not used to such honesty. I like it. What does VJ stand for?" he asked and propped his chin on a palm, letting his gaze roam over her expressive face. Women were manipulative and scheming where he came from. This one was different.

"Victoria Jane. It's too fancy for these parts, so folks mostly call me VJ."

VJ fit her—it was short, sassy and unusual. "Most? But not all?"

"Perceptive, aren't you? My mom didn't. But she's been gone now almost a year."

Ouch. The pain flickering through her eyes drilled right through him, leaving a gaping hole. Before thinking it through, he reached out and gently enfolded her hand in his.

"I'm sorry," he said. After the ill-fated exchange of harsh words with his father sixteen years ago, Kris had walked away from a guaranteed position at Demetrious Shipping, the Demetrious fortune and Greece entirely. His relationship with his mom had been one of the casualties, and phone calls weren't the same. But he couldn't imagine a world where even a call wasn't possible. "That must've been tough. Must still be."

"Are you trying to make me cry?" She swallowed hard.

Dishes clinked and clacked from the kitchen and the noise split the air.

"Pearl's subtle way of telling me to get my butt to work." VJ rolled wet, shiny eyes. "Honestly, she should pick up your check. This place hasn't seen such a big crowd since Old Man Smith's funeral."

While he'd been distracted, locals had packed the place. Most of the tables were now full of nuclear families, worn-out men in crusty boots or acne-faced teenagers.

"So you're saying I'm at least as popular as a dead man?" It shouldn't have been funny, but the corners of his mouth twitched none the less.

Soberly, she pulled her hand from his and stood. Her natural friendliness had returned and then vanished. He missed it.

"Well, I have to work." She eased away, her expression blank. "Nice to meet you, Mr. Demetrious. I wish you and Ms. Monroe all the happiness in the world with your upcoming marriage."

He scowled. "Kyla and I aren't engaged."

Yet. It didn't improve his mood to hear rumors of the impending engagement had already surfaced, courtesy of Kyla, no doubt.

Why was this still bothering him? He'd agreed to give Kyla a ring. The deal was done if he wanted to make *Visions of Black*. He entertained no romantic illusions about love or marriage. Marriage based on a business agreement had a better chance of succeeding than one based on anything else. Of course, he was never going to marry anyone, least of all Kyla, whom he hadn't even seen in a couple of months, not since she'd called off their relationship in a fit of tears and theatrical moaning. At which point she'd likely jumped right back into bed with Guy Hansen.

"Oh. Well, then, have a nice life instead." VJ smiled and bounced to the kitchen.

At least he'd been able to improve her mood.

Later that night, VJ grinned as she walked up the listing steps to the house, jumped the broken one and cracked the screen door silently.

Kris and Kyla Monroe weren't engaged.

Oh, it made no difference in the grand scheme of things, but she couldn't stop smiling regardless. He was compassionate, sinfully hot and a little more available than she'd assumed.

Was there *anything* wrong with him? If so, she didn't want to know. For now, he was her fantasy, with no faults and no bad habits.

It was fun to imagine Kris returning for her someday, top down on the Ferrari and a handful of red roses. And it was slightly depressing since it would never happen in a million years. He was on his way to Dallas and that would be that.

She tiptoed into the hallway and froze when a board creaked. Dang it, she never missed that one.

"Girl, is that you?" Daddy's slurred voice shot out from the living room.

She winced. Angry drunk tonight. What had happened this time to set him off?

Her stomach plummeted. The part. She'd forgotten all about the part for Gus's truck, and it was still sitting in the cab of Daddy's truck. Her head had been full of Kristian Demetrious, with no room for anything else.

She put some starch in her spine and walked into the living room. Her father slumped in the same armchair where he had taken residence earlier in the afternoon. His eyes were bloodshot, swollen.

"Lookee here." Daddy took a swig of beer and backhanded his mouth with his knuckles. "Finally decided to prance your butt home, didja?"

He looked bad. They'd all dealt with Mama's death in their own way, but Daddy wasn't dealing with it at all, falling farther into a downward, drunken spiral every day.

"I'm sorry about the part, Daddy. I got to town late," she hedged. "I had to go straight to work."

"Gus needs his truck. You get over there and fix it now," he commanded, then downed the rest of his beer and belched. He set the empty can on the closest table without looking.

It teetered on the edge, and then fell to the floor with a clank. Beer dribbled onto the hardwood floor, creating another mess to clean up.

"It's late. Bobby Junior can fix it in the morning." Along with everything else since he was running the garage in their father's stead.

Guilt panged her breastbone. Bobby Junior had a wife and three kids he never saw. What else did she have to do? Lie in bed and dream about a Greek god who was speeding away toward a life that did not, and never would, include her?

Daddy bobbled the TV remote into his paw. "I told you to do it. Ungrateful hussy. Bring me another beer, would ya?"

Her head snapped up and anger swept the guilt aside. "Daddy, you're drunk and you need to go to bed, so I'll forgive you for calling me that."

"Don't you raise your voice to me, missy!" He weaved to his feet and shook the remote. "And don't you pass judgment down your prissy little nose, either. I ain't drunk. I'm hungry because you ran off and forgot about cooking me dinner. Your job is here."

"Sorry, Daddy. I don't mean to be disrespectful." She bit her lip and pushed on. "But I'm moving to Dallas soon, like I've been telling you for months. You and the boys have to figure out how to do things for yourselves."

Jenny Porter's cousin was buying a condo and had offered to rent the extra bedroom to VJ, but it wasn't built yet and wouldn't be until September. Fall couldn't get here fast enough.

Daddy shook his head. "The Good Lord put women on this earth to cook, clean and have a man's babies. You can do that right here in Little Crooked Creek."

"I'm not staying here to enable you to drink yourself into the grave." Her dry eyes burned. "I'm tired. I'm sorry about Gus's truck and for forgetting your dinner. But I'm done here." She turned and took a step toward her room.

Daddy's fingernails bit into her upper arm as he spun her and yanked until her face was inches from his. "Don't you turn your back on me, girl." Alcohol-laced breath gushed from his mouth and turned her stomach with its stench. "You'll quit your job and forget about running off to live in that devil's den."

He emphasized each word with a shake that rattled her entire body. Tears sprang up as he squeezed the forming bruises. For the first time since her mother's death, she was genuinely afraid of her father and what he might do. Mama had always been the referee. Her lone defender and supporter in a household of males. VJ didn't have her mother's patience or her saintly ability to overlook Daddy's faults.

If she could escape to her room, she could grab some clothes and dash over to Pamela Sue's house.

"Thought you were pretty smart hiding all that money under the bed in your unmentionables box," he said.

It took her a second. "You were snooping in my room?"

She jerked her arm free as panic flitted up her back. Surely he hadn't looked inside the tampon box. Her brothers wouldn't have touched it with a ten-foot pole, and she'd been smugly certain it was the perfect hiding place.

"This is my house and so's everything in it. Needed me a new truck. Tackle got it in El Paso today." Her father smirked and nodded toward the rear of the house.

The room tilted as she looked out the back window. In the driveway of the detached garage sat a brand-new truck with paper plates.

"You stole my money? All of it?" Her lungs collapsed and breath whooshed out, strangling her.

"My house, so it's my money."

Her money was gone.

She could have opened an account at Sweetwater Bank where Aunt Mary worked after all. Then Daddy might have found out about the money but wouldn't have been able to touch it. Hindsight.

What was she going to do? Most of the money had been Mama's, slipped to VJ on the sly when her prognosis had turned bad. It would take at least a week to earn enough at Pearl's to buy a bus ticket. Never mind eating or any other basic necessities. Like rent.

Numb to the bone, she blurted, "My money, so it's my truck. Give me the keys." She held out a palm and tried to remember what Daddy had been like before Mama died, but that man was long gone.

He guffawed. "The keys are hid good, and it's got anti-theft, so don't even think about hot-wiring it. Now that you see how things are gonna go, getcher butt in the kitchen and fix me something to eat."

"No, Daddy. You've gone too far. Do it yourself."

A blow knocked her to the side, almost off her feet. Tiny needles of pain swept the surface of her cheek. She'd never seen the cuff coming.

"I'm tired of your mouth, girl. While you're in the kitchen, clean up a little, too, why don't ya? The boys left dishes in the sink." He fell into the recliner as if nothing had changed.

Her cheekbone began to throb, overshadowing the painful bruising on her arm by quadruple. She had to get away. Now was her chance.

She sprinted to her room, ignoring her father's bellowing. Her body felt heavy, almost too heavy to move. Once inside her room, she threw her weight against the door. After two tries, she wedged a chair under the knob good enough to stay upright, but not good enough to hold off a drunken rage if her father had a mind to follow her.

Numb, she stumbled around the room throwing things into a bag. Lots of things, as many as it would hold, because she wasn't coming back. She couldn't spend a couple of nights at Pamela Sue's house and wait until Daddy sobered up like usual.

She tore out of her waitress uniform, ripping a sleeve in the process, but it hardly mattered since she'd never wear it again. Her father had been right—she would quit her job, but not because he said so. Because she was leaving. Without glancing at them, she pulled on a T-shirt and jeans, blinking hard so the tears would stay inside.

Abandoning Mama's collection of romance novels almost killed her, but five hundred paperbacks lined the bookshelf. Maybe someday she could come back for them or ask Bobby Junior to ship them to her, but they'd likely be thrown out before she had the money for something that expensive. She couldn't leave behind *Embrace the Rogue* and slipped it into the overstuffed bag. It had been Mama's favorite.

A crash reverberated from the other side of the door.

Quickly, she yanked the curtain aside and threw up the window. With the heel of her hand, she popped off the screen and flung a leg over the windowsill, careful not to look back at the sanctuary she'd called hers since the day she was born. Her courage was only as strong as the sting across her face and when it faded, she feared reason would return.

She had nowhere to go, no money and a broken heart.

VJ started walking toward Main and got about halfway to Pearl's before the tears threatened again. Two deep, shuddery breaths, then another two, socked the tears away. She didn't have the luxury of grief. Other folks made a career out of drama and hardship, but none of that nonsense paid the bills. Only firm resolve got things done.

Twenty-six dollars in tips lay folded in her pocket, a windfall on most days. The crowd had been thick, thanks to lightning-quick word of mouth about the fancy foreign car in Pearl's parking lot.

Twenty-six dollars would barely cover a day's worth of meals at the cheapest fast-food restaurant, if by some miracle she could hitch a ride to Van Horn anonymously. Everyone for fifty miles knew her and would tattle to Daddy before breakfast. He'd come after her for sure if that happened.

The school she'd attended for twelve years loomed ahead, ghosts of those years dancing in the weak moonlight illuminating the playground. The next building on the block was the garage, and the sight of it almost changed her mind. Lenny and Billy would only miss her at meal time, but Bobby Junior and Tackle depended on her to pitch in around the shop.

Then again, Tackle had bought the truck for Daddy. Surely he'd asked where the money had come from. Daddy could have lied, but her brother's probable betrayal hollowed out her insides.

She passed MacIntyre's Drugstore. No more hanging out there with Pamela Sue at the lunch counter.

The end of things would have come soon enough once the condo in Dallas was built, but that was later. This was now, and it was harder than she'd expected.

Mercifully, there were no buildings on Main past the drugstore for a quarter of a mile. She finally reached the one and only motel in Little Crooked Creek and rehearsed some lines designed to talk her way into a free room.

A flash of yellow drove everything out of her mind.

Moonlight glinted off the *muy amarilla* Ferrari parked under the lone streetlight. Her pulse hammered in her throat. Kris was still here. Not driving toward Dallas and Kyla, to whom he wasn't engaged.

It was fate.

Maybe he'd give her a ride in exchange for directions. He'd defended her against her brothers. He would help her, she knew he would.

But then she'd have to explain what happened to her money and why the big hurry to get out of town. She ground her teeth. Kris didn't need to be burdened with her soap opera. Neither did she want to lie.

What if she made it seem like she was helping him? What if something was mysteriously wrong with the car?

Oh, it won't start? Let me look at it. Ah, here's the problem. No, I couldn't accept anything in return. Except maybe a ride to Dallas.

Stupid plan. *It's a Ferrari, dummy, not a Ford.* What if the engine was different than the domestic ones she knew?

There was only one way to find out and what else did she have? Not money. Not choices. Here was a golden opportunity to escape Little Crooked Creek forever and start over in Dallas. Her future roommate would surely take her in a little early, allowing VJ to crash on her couch. Once she got on her feet, she'd pay Beverly back, with interest.

Holy cow, the trip to Dallas was like nine hours. Nine hours in the company of Kristian Demetrious. Five hundred and forty minutes. More, if she could stretch it out.

She peered into the interior of the car, careful not to touch the glass in case the alarm was supersonic. The dash was devoid of blinking red lights, which hopefully meant no alarm at all. She fished a metal nail file from her purse and frowned. Not nearly long enough to pop the lock from the outside. Maybe she could peel the convertible top back a little and stick the file in that way.

On a hunch, she tried the handle. The door swung open easily. Unlocked. Only the rich.

Quickly, she released the deck lid and beelined it to the rear of the car. At least she knew the engine was in the back instead of for the front. But it was downright foreign, an engine for a space ship instead of for a car, but one mechanism was the same. She reached in and wiggled the ignition coil wire loose.

Now nothing would start this car without her help. She

closed the deck lid with a quiet click and retrieved her bag. Now, where to wait for Kris?

Wrinkling her nose at the space next to the Dumpster, she settled onto the concrete by the ice machine and tried to relax enough to fall asleep. Not likely with the knowledge this was probably the first of many nights sleeping on the street.

This plan had to work. Had to. Heavy, humid air pressed down on her in the dark silence. Crickets chirped in the field beside the motel, but the music did nothing to take her mind off the panic rolling around in her stomach.

What if Kris wasn't meant to be her knight in shining armor?

Three

Kris examined the engine of Kyla's car. Nothing seemed out of place, but how would he know if it was? The Ferrari had started fine every time he'd driven it. Why had it picked now, and here, to flake out?

Penance, for the delay. That's why. Kyla had undoubtedly cursed it, then texted him to bring it to her in Dallas, pretty please. He should have shipped the car instead of driving it. She wouldn't have cared either way, but no. He'd driven to allow time to obsess over the inflexible Hollywood machine. Muttering slurs on Italian engineers, he yanked his phone out of his back pocket.

"Car problems, chief?" VJ's honeyed drawl rang out from behind him.

He grinned, strangely elated, and twisted to greet her. Whatever he'd been about to say died in his throat.

With a succinct curse, he ran a thumb over the welt on her upper cheek. "What happened to your face?"

She flinched and turned away, but he hooked a finger under

her chin and guided her face into the sunlight. The injury wasn't bad enough to need medical attention but quick-burning rage flared up behind his rib cage nonetheless.

"Who did that to you?" he demanded. "One of your brothers?"

She better start naming names really fast before he tore this town apart, redneck by redneck, until someone else spilled. VJ was small, so small. How could anyone strike her with force hard enough to bruise?

"Nobody. I tripped." She shifted her gaze to the ground and pulled her chin from his fingers. "It was dark."

"Right."

The maids rearranged the furniture again, my darling, his mother used to say. Regardless of the continent, the excuses were equally as ineffective, as if he was both blind and stupid. This time, he wasn't a scared kid, hiding in his room, creating stories in his head where he controlled what the characters did and it all turned out happy in the end.

Fury curled his hands into fists. He'd never been able to help his mother, distancing himself further and further from a powerless situation. Distancing himself from the rage, the only defense he had against turning into his father.

His parents had been madly, passionately in love once upon a time and their relationship had degenerated into ugliness Kris refused to duplicate. So now he employed strict compensation mechanisms: avoiding confrontation, avoiding serious relationships and staying detached. Women got sick of it fast, which he accepted. Maybe even encouraged. Kyla had been no exception.

Now, it was too late to disengage and even he wasn't good enough to pretend indifference. VJ needed his help. Like it or not, his role in this had a second act.

"Really," she said, refusing to meet his eyes. "It was an accident. Can I help you with the car?"

"An accident." He crossed his arms and stared down at her. "What did you trip over?"

"Uh, the couch."

He nodded to the ugly blotch on her arm, which wrapped around her biceps in the shape of a hand, with half-moon cuts at the top of the purple fingers. "Did the couch have hands with fingernails?"

Her face crumpled, and he spit out a curse. Panicked, he enfolded her into his arms, determined to do something, anything to help.

Then he remembered VJ barely knew him. She'd smack him with her bag for being so familiar.

But she didn't. Instead she snuggled into his chest, sobbing. Her head fit into the hollow of his breastbone as if it had been shaped for her, and VJ's slight frame kick-started a fiercely possessive, protective instinct. He tightened his arms and inhaled the coconut scent of her warm cinnamon-colored hair.

After a minute, the bawling stopped. She wiggled away and took a deep breath. Her face was mottled and wet. She swiped at it with the hem of her giant T-shirt, this one with a cracked emblem for Tres Hombres Automotive Distributing, and looked up. "I'm sorry. I don't know where that came from."

"I do," he said grimly. "You've had a rough night, which wasn't helped by sleeping outside. Let me take you somewhere, as long as it's not back to whoever hit you."

"I didn't sleep outside," she protested. "I'm on my way to work. That's the only reason I'm out this early."

"You have a concrete-patterned print down the side of your face. The other side," he clarified as she tentatively touched the bruises. She obviously had no clue how much practice he had in seeing through a woman's lies. Normally, he'd be infuriated with her attempt at deception, but instead, the urge to take action, to fix things for her, unfolded.

"Get in the car." He swore, colorfully, but mindful enough of the offensive content to do it in Greek. "I forgot. Something's wrong with the car. Can you give me the number to your garage?"

Out of nowhere, she burst into tears again.

He rubbed her shoulder and said the first thing that came to mind, "I'm sorry. That wasn't a dig at your mechanical skills. I'd love it if you'd look at my car. Please."

"Don't apologize," she grumbled, sniffling. "That only makes it worse."

"Um, this seems to be the sole situation where it's wrong for a guy to apologize. Can you possibly explain what wouldn't be wrong to say?"

Without a word, she skirted him and leaned into the engine bay. With a couple of skillful twists, she reattached a loose wire he hadn't noticed and she mumbled, "I disconnected it last night. Try it now."

Speechless, he slid into the driver's seat and pushed the start button. With a meaty roar, the engine sprang to life. The RPM needle flicked back and forth with each nudge of the accelerator.

He vaulted out of the seat and rounded the back end before she fled.

"*Now* get in the car."

"I can't." Misery pulled at her expression. "This is all wrong. I'm sorry. I had a stupid plan to trade fixing your car for a ride, but it wouldn't have needed fixing if I hadn't sabotaged it. Then you had to be all nice and wonderful and understanding about my…" She waved a flustered hand at her bruises. "Problems. I'm a terrible person, and I can't take advantage of you."

Kris bit his lip so the bubble of laughter wouldn't burst out. "Let me get this straight. You can't accept a ride because you don't want to take advantage of me."

"Your hospitality," she amended quickly. "I don't want to take advantage of your hospitality. Or take advantage in any other way. Not that you're repulsive or anything. I mean, I would take advantage if I had the opportunity. You're totally hot." She hissed out a little moan, and he yearned to hear it again. "That didn't come out right. Can I crawl in a hole now?"

"No." He crossed his arms and leaned a hip on the side panel. Was it terrible to be charmed by how negotiating a simple ride tore her up? "It's too late. You've already admitted you can't be trusted with my virtue. Whatever will I do?"

She glared at him but then her expression wavered. "I do have a reputation in the greater Little Crooked Creek area. Mothers have been known to lock up their sons when they see me coming."

Her humor and winsome self-deprecation was back, loosening the bands around his lungs. "Well, my mother is six thousand miles away so I guess I'll have to risk it. Let's try this. I'll forgive you for sabotaging the car if you'll forgive me for not believing you tripped." Smoothly, he captured her hand and led her to the passenger side. He opened the door. "Shall we?"

She didn't climb in. Staring at their joined hands, she said, "Yesterday morning you were blissfully unaware I existed. Why do you want to get mixed up in this?"

A fair question, but the wrong one. His involvement had begun the moment she pulled off the highway and ensnared him, forcing him into the action.

A better question was how long he'd stay involved.

"Is someone going to come after me with a shotgun?"

"I doubt it." She snorted out a laugh. "Bobby Junior and Tackle might consider it, but they're too busy. The cretins... sorry. My other brothers would have to notice I was gone first."

"What about your father?"

Shadows sprang into her eyes and her grip tightened. He had his name.

"I honestly can't say what Daddy would do. That's the best reason of all for you to forget about me and drive away as fast as you can."

"You've obviously mistaken me for someone without a conscience. I couldn't sleep at night if I did that. Get in the car, VJ."

"How can you be real?" She studied his face, the same as she had last night, as if looking for the answers to her deepest questions. "It's like I dreamed up the perfect man and poof, here you are."

It should be a crime to be that naive. He dropped her hand. "I'm far from perfect. If you get in the car, you'll doubtlessly find out I'm not always a fun date. Don't turn me into some altruistic saint because I'm offering you a ride."

She hesitated, then nodded once. "Okay. I'll take the ride, but I'm allowed to worship you in secret or no deal."

The bruising on her face stood out in sharp relief against her fragile skin yet when the corners of her mouth flipped up in a small smile, he couldn't help but smile, too. "How could I turn that down?"

He helped her into the passenger seat and slammed the door. She slumped against the leather, and even through the tinted glass, she radiated an aura that pinged around inside him, seeking a place to land.

Dangerous, that's what she was. When was the last time he'd willingly tossed away his stay-detached rule?

Once settled behind the wheel, he slipped on his sunglasses and said, "I've already checked out, so where would you like me to take you? Your girlfriend's house, the one from last night?"

She stared out the window, pointedly not looking at him. "I'm afraid it's a little more complicated than that."

VJ flat-handed sunglasses against her face and debated how to explain she was going to Dallas without coming across as a freeloader, or worse, a stalker.

Her only plan had died the second Kris held her and let her cry on his fifty-dollar T-shirt. How was she going to convince him to let her tag along when she had nothing to give him in return? Well, nothing other than an annoying set of calf eyes, cowardice disguised as automotive expertise and twenty-six dollars, twenty of which Kris had tipped her in the first place.

"Complicated is my specialty," he commented mildly and

drove to the motel lot exit. His graceful fingers draped over the wheel casually, as if he was so in tune with the car, it anticipated his bidding instead of relying on mere mechanical direction. "Right or left?"

She inhaled sharply and the scent of new car and fresh leather hit her like a freight train. A fitting combination for a new start.

Might as well go for broke.

"Left and then another right at the Feed and Seed. Go about five hundred miles and then another right. That'll put me pretty close to where I want to go."

"Ah." He nodded sagely and slapped a palm to his chest, Pledge of Allegiance style. "A woman after my own heart. You're running away. Why didn't you say so?"

Because running away sounded so juvenile, especially out of his mouth.

"Am I that transparent?"

"Yeah." That slow, sexy smile spread across his face. "Don't worry, I like it."

"Hmmpf. I'd rather be a woman of mystery and secrets."

"No, you wouldn't." His gaze shifted to the highway and stayed there. "You just think you would. Secretive women are irritating."

He meant someone specific. Her curiosity spiked, but the firm set of his mouth said *don't ask*. So she bit her tongue and mirrored his feigned fascination with the road stretched ahead through the windshield. Little Crooked Creek fell away at a rapid pace. Good riddance.

After a while, she might miss someone or something other than Pamela Sue, Bobby Junior and Tackle. Mama's grave. Pearl probably. The sunset against a mountain backdrop.

For now, the call of adventure and a new life drowned out whispers of the past.

Kris nodded toward the floorboard, where a broken-in black

leather bag was wedged under the dash. "Find my MP3 player and pick out some music. It's a long drive to Dallas."

"You're going to take me?" She'd been studiously avoiding the subject, hoping to segue back into it later. Like after it was too late to turn around.

"You're in the car, and I'm driving to Dallas. Seems like that's going to be the end result."

Relief lessened the weight on her shoulders. Nine hours in the company of Kris. Nine hours in an amazing car with her Greek god in shining armor. It wasn't nearly long enough, but far more than she deserved. "You aren't mad?"

With a half laugh, he said, "About what? Didn't we go through this already?"

Sinking low in the seat, she tried to make herself as small as possible. "Because I wasn't honest with you. I practically forced you into taking on an unwanted passenger."

After a beat of silence, he tapped the steering wheel in a staccato rhythm. "I drink coffee black, I refuse to screw the lid on the toothpaste when I'll have to take it back off again, and no one—*no one*—can force me to do something I don't want to do." A wealth of pain and untold history underpinned the sentiments, darkening his tone. She hated being responsible for bringing back bad memories. "Now you know the three most important things about me. Next time, ask instead of making assumptions."

Her fantasy gained dimensions and layers. And she craved more depth, more knowledge, more understanding of this extraordinary person in the next seat.

"Oh, no. You busted my deal all to pieces. I can't worship someone who doesn't screw the lid back on the toothpaste." She shook her head and tsked. "That's wrong. What if it gets lost?"

His million-dollar smile burst into place, and she intended to keep it there. It was the one repayment she could give him. Of course, it was a win-win in her book.

"Lost? I throw it away. Waste of plastic."

"Figures."

The craving intensified. What kind of music did he listen to? She hooked the bag and pulled it into her lap, then rifled through it, absorbing, touching. These were Kris's personal belongings. A green toothbrush. A stick of deodorant. A brush with a black stretchy band twisted around the handle. She'd never seen him with his hair tied back and hoped she never did. His loose, shoulder-length style was nothing short of mouthwatering.

"Having trouble finding it?" he asked a touch sarcastically, as if he knew she was a heartbeat from inhaling the citrusy scent of his deodorant.

"I confess. I'm actually a reporter for a celebrity magazine doing an expose on independent film directors. And their luggage." She was rambling. Spitting out whatever came to her mind because her fingers had closed around a small, square box with a hinged lid that every woman on the planet could identify. Blindfolded. "You caught me."

She dropped the ring box, but her hand still stung. Why did an engagement ring in the bag of a man she'd just met put a lump in her throat? So he wasn't engaged to Kyla yet, but obviously it was only a matter of time. Better all the way around to accept that he was completely unavailable. Much, much better. Then she could make a clean break. Wipe him from her mind once he left her in Dallas.

He glanced at her over the top of his sunglasses. "What's wrong?"

"Nothing's wrong." She yanked the only electronic device from the bottom of the bag and waved it, hoping it wasn't a newfangled garage-door opener. "Got it. Let's see what we have here. How do I turn it on?"

"You've never used an MP3 player?" Amusement colored his question. "Touch the screen to wake it up."

"It's asleep?" Fascinated, she flipped the gizmo over and right-side up again. "Does it snore and hog all the covers, too?"

His rich laughter washed over her and she wallowed in it. He reached over, slid a fingertip across the device and colors illuminated the screen. Colors she barely registered because his arm pressed against her shoulder, sparking like a firecracker in a Coke bottle as he deftly tapped the MP3 player.

The brush of body parts was totally innocent but the pang low in her belly unleashed a flood of longing more akin to original sin.

"There's the song list," he offered nonchalantly. "Pick one."

She glanced down at the screen, contracting her diaphragm until she could speak again. "I don't know any of these artists." Was that her voice? She cleared her throat and prayed it eliminated the huskiness. "Any Kenny Chesney or Miranda Lambert?"

Nope, still croaking like a late-night ad for a 1-900 number.

"There's no country music on this and there's not going to be." He took the player from her and stuck it in the holder on the dash. Two taps later, a stringed instrument wailed through the speakers, the melody so instantly heartbreaking, it stole her breath. She'd never imagined such passion could be poured into music.

"The musician is Johannes Linstead," he said. "Do you like it?"

"It's so beautiful, it hurts my chest. Is it weird that it makes me feel like weeping?"

With two fingers, he slid off his sunglasses and impaled her with stormy, liquid eyes, searching her face with an immeasurable intensity. "The music makes me feel like that, too."

She couldn't break their locked gazes. Didn't want to. A whole other world lived inside his eyes, a world she wanted to fall into.

"It'll be our secret," he whispered and snapped his attention back to the road as he obscured his eyes with the sunglasses again.

Her heart beat so fast, she was shocked it wasn't audible.

She stared at his profile. What had just happened? It had been A Charged Moment. Thrilling—for her, at least. But what did it mean?

She might be from Nowheresville but she could follow instructions. "Instead of assuming again, I'm going to ask. Why does it seem like you're flirting with me sometimes?"

"I am."

"Why?" Additional words, phrases, ideas escaped her. In fact, it had been a surprise her tongue worked at all.

"Why not?" He lifted a shoulder. "I like you. You're fun. Beautiful."

He thought she was beautiful? The jumpy crickets stampeded through her stomach.

Stuff like this didn't happen to her. Oh, she'd had her share of boyfriends—small-town, small-minded boys who wouldn't know romance if it bit them in their unimaginative butts.

The difference between them and this enthralling, charming man beside her was the difference between Ford and Ferrari.

But he wasn't finished. "What does it hurt? It's harmless and has zero calories. Besides, you're flirting back."

Harmless. Nothing more than sport for the beautiful people. Yes, Kristian Demetrious was exactly like his car. Smooth, exotic and his engine was equally unfathomable.

The crickets died a quick death. "Of course I'm flirting back. You're driving. I'd hate to be dumped on the side of the road."

He paused for a beat and didn't laugh. "Women don't flirt with me. They slip me room keys and follow me into the bathroom. Flirting with you is the polar opposite of that. I enjoy it. There aren't any expectations. It's safe."

Now she was safe. How appealing.

She needed to throw it in reverse, distance herself, or eventually he'd drive right over her heart, flattening it like an unfortunate armadillo too transfixed by the bright lights of the freeway to see the splat coming. "Tell me about Kyla. Where did you meet her?"

He glowered, tightening the lines of his cheeks and mouth, and the expression looked wrong on him. "I don't want to talk about Kyla."

The reference to his glamorous soon-to-be fiancée was like a shock of icy water. The atmosphere in the car cooled and grew icicles. Fantastic. Exactly as she'd intended. Now she wasn't thinking about that seething, charged moment. Or the sparkling weight of his arm against hers.

"Well, I don't want to talk about Kyla, either. Tell me about your next movie." That should be an innocuous enough subject, and she'd been dying to revisit it after seeing his entire demeanor transform upon mentioning it at Pearl's.

"I'd rather not talk for a while."

She flinched at the bite in his tone. "Sure. No problem."

The less they talked, the better, because then his beyond-sexy accent wouldn't skim down her spine and take up residence inside, heating every pore of her skin as if she'd crawled into the sun.

They barely knew each other. They were strangers soon to part ways and only thrown together because she lacked the fortitude to leave Little Crooked Creek on her own. What else could they possibly be to each other?

Road signs for Van Horn flashed by twice before Kris sighed. "Sorry. I can be a jerk."

She waved dismissively. "Don't apologize for not wanting me to pry into your life. I'm sure people do that all the time, and you'd like to keep some things private."

"That's true, but it's not the reason I'm a jerk. It's complicated."

"Complicated is my specialty."

He grinned and shot her another of those enigmatic glances over the top of his sunglasses. "Have I mentioned how much I like you?"

"Yes, but you should definitely tell me again." Maybe she was getting better at the sport of flirting. The trick was not to let on how that kind of statement thrummed straight to the place between her thighs.

He bit his lip, contemplating. She had to avert her eyes from the sight of his white teeth sinking into flesh.

"The problem is," he said, "Kyla's starring in my next film, *Visions of Black*. I guess I'm kind of touchy about it because of the unconventional demands around the financing. Without the right backing, the project's dead. The downside of not being affiliated with a studio."

"Contract negotiations are shaky. I get it. Is it worth whatever your investor is demanding?"

He froze, and her hand flew to his arm before she'd realized it. She wanted to comfort him but had no idea why.

She did know one thing—Kris wasn't and never would be a stranger. There was something between them. A recognition. A mystical draw she couldn't ignore or pretend to have imagined.

"Is it worth it?" He exhaled and nodded slowly. "To have a chance to direct this film, which will solidify my career and put me on the A-list? Yes, it is. I've been busting my back for years to get this shot."

The raw longing and aspiration carved into his expression hit her in a wave way hotter than the music. She swallowed, hard. Her fantasy imploded and shrank down to one crystalline shard of desire—that he'd look at her like that. She tucked it away before it grew too sharp.

"That's a lot of mileage for one film." No doubt he'd be successful, as soon as his investor was happy. "Out of curiosity, what is he asking you to do?"

A tiny muscle in his forehead jumped. "Announce that Kyla and I are engaged."

Four

Kris could have gone at least another hundred miles without mentioning that. Next he'd be telling VJ it was all a publicity stunt, one he strongly suspected Kyla had talked Abrams into as a method to either push her way into Kris's bed again or drive him insane. Maybe both. Kris assumed she'd split with Guy Hansen and was on the hunt for another warm, male body, but, knowing Kyla, she could have other ulterior motives. Until he figured out her agenda, it was better to stay off the subject.

Regardless of who had devised the fake engagement, he recognized the value of Kyla's attachment to *Visions* and had to suck it up. Without her in the starring role and without the publicity, Abrams would pull out. Without Abrams's experience making blockbusters, Kris's career couldn't move to the next level. Period.

"Oh." As if fascinated, VJ stared out the window at the landscape dotted with lumpy cactus and heat shimmers, which she'd doubtlessly seen a million times.

VJ was at a loss for words. That was unfortunate, but the less said about Kyla and engagements, the better.

"Hungry?" he asked.

She shook her head. "No. Thanks."

"Is that your wallet talking or your stomach?" He glanced at her, certain it was the former. He'd never met someone so determined not to accept nice gestures.

Her forehead scrunched. "Are you practicing your ESP?"

"Yeah." He turned back to the road. "For my next trick, I'm going to levitate."

The joke went over like his last film, with zero reaction and a lot of white knuckles. Where had all the fun and flirting gone? From the moment VJ appeared out of a swirl of dust, the awful temper he'd been in since leaving L.A. had fled and he didn't want it to come back.

After a few minutes of silence so loud his eardrums hurt, she said, "So. Kyla's a lucky woman. I'm sure you'll be really happy together. How are you going to propose to her? Put the ring in a champagne glass?" Her tone was bright and saccharine-fake.

Kyla had her spooked. Inexplicably, he opened his mouth to tell her that he and Kyla had split up a while ago. But, he closed it. He valued his relationship with Jack Abrams and hoped to partner on many more films with the man. VJ probably wouldn't tell but accidents happened and his job was to drive positive press. Not put the smile back on the face of his desert mirage. "I haven't thought about it. I'll probably give her the ring and ask."

VJ gaped. "You can't do that. It's a *proposal,* not asking her to dinner at a dress-up place. She's dreamed of it her entire life. It has to be perfect. Something she can tell your kids and grandkids over and over because it's so outrageously romantic. You have to do better."

"Are you kidding? You've never met Kyla, I realize. But come on." He downshifted to go around a slow-moving cattle truck.

She flipped a spiral of cinnamon hair over her shoulder. "You don't think she's dreamed about her one and only proposal her whole life?"

One and only? Huge disparity in world views there. Kyla had already been married once to an Australian actor, a fact VJ's celebrity magazines had clearly omitted. Before he could mention it, he suddenly envisioned stepping on puppies. Treading lightly might be a better idea than squashing her idealism. "Have you?"

"Of course! Like a million times."

Her face took on the glow he'd been missing and his gut clenched. His reaction to her was so pure and elemental, with no expectations. Which was why he enjoyed it—no danger of it going anywhere. So she was the romantic sort, envisioning her new last name and assigning genders to her unborn children. Delusions which led to heartbreak when the passion faded. Figured.

While nothing about relationships made for his favorite topic of discussion, if he got to bask in VJ's fresh smile, he could buck up. "Tell me."

"About my dream proposal?"

"You've imagined it a million times. Should be easy."

Leather squealed as she sank down into the seat. If he didn't know better, he'd think she was trying to disappear into it. "You'll think it's stupid."

"No, I won't." His curiosity flared. Ever since he'd mentioned the engagement stunt, she'd withdrawn. He wanted her in-your-face honesty back. "I want to know. Everything about you interests me."

She shot him a sidelong glance behind her sunglasses. "You're not allowed to laugh, okay?"

"No chance."

She took a deep breath. "I want to get my engagement ring as a present in a huge box, so I don't guess what's in it. When I open it, the little box will be inside. Then I'd realize."

That was the proposal she'd imagined a million times? "Sounds very nice."

And boring. A hundred scenarios sprang to mind, all of which eclipsed that in terms of romantic proposals. In seconds, the entire scene unfolded in his head and he started dropping in thematic elements like roses and soft lighting. Maybe that was the key to the theme for *Visions of Black*—lighting.

"Beats the one I got."

She'd done it again. Pulled him out from behind the lens with an intriguing statement. "Someone proposed to you?"

"Walt Phillips." Her lip curled. "It wasn't really a proposal. More of a statement. Like it was foregone we'd get married because we'd been dating since high school. How long have you and Kyla been together?"

Back to that again. "I don't know." He tapped the steering wheel with restless fingers. "I don't pay attention to stuff like that."

"You don't celebrate anniversaries?"

"There's more than one?"

"Anniversary of your first date, anniversary of your first kiss. The first time you made love, the first time you…" She trailed off as he raised an eyebrow. "What?"

Nobody kept track of those milestones. "Nothing. Are you sure you don't want breakfast?"

"Are you sure you want to marry someone you aren't in love with?"

The car veered toward the center line and he overcorrected, shooting the passenger-side tires past the white line of the shoulder, jouncing them both until he got the wheel under control. Precisely the reason he stayed behind the camera—so he couldn't be caught off guard. "Seems like you're the one practicing ESP. What makes you think I'm not in love with Kyla?"

"Please." She snorted. "I don't need ESP to know you're not in love with her. Even if you are from Hollywood, you wouldn't be flirting with me if you were. You'd remember the first time you kissed her. The first time you held her all night. You wouldn't be able to stand being separated from her, yet this car's got a V-8 and you're barely driving the speed limit. Doesn't take a rocket scientist to do the math."

He bit back a nervous laugh. He'd been angling to get her smart mouth back. Just not with that much punch. "Would you like to drive since I'm doing such a poor job?"

"Deflection. Yet another obvious factor. You don't even like to talk about Kyla."

While he might prefer to stay behind the camera, VJ never let him retreat. Women usually gave up trying to engage him after several unsuccessful rounds. VJ didn't have to try—she was naturally engaging. With renewed respect, he eyed her. "Maybe because my relationship with her is private."

"Or because you don't have much of a relationship. Marriage is forever. You should only marry someone you're desperately in love with. Someone you can't live without."

Actually, he'd be ecstatic to be desperately in *like* with Kyla. They were going to be spending a lot of time together, after all, filming the movie and doing public appearances. At some point, he should probably tell Kyla he didn't hold the affair with Guy against her. He still stewed about it occasionally, but only because Hansen was an idiot.

"That's not love, that's passion. Which is all hormones anyway and I can't think of a worse reason to marry someone. Passion dies."

And when it died, it ruined everything.

"Are you looped?" she asked. "Love and passion are tied together and the *only* reason to marry someone. Clearly, your education is lacking in the romance department."

She stroked his arm and it wasn't accidental. His eyes unfocused as heat radiated from the contact of her fingers. His groin tightened. Again.

Not only did VJ keep him engaged, she poked at something

elemental inside. In the past, attraction had led to satisfaction, not this raw yearning for…more.

"Oh, I see," he said when his mouth stopped being too dry to talk. "You're an expert on romance."

"I am, actually." She seemed pleased with his insight. "We have hours to kill until we reach Dallas. I'll be happy to give you some instruction."

Romance instruction at the hands of Victoria Jane. The idea should have been hilarious. It wasn't. "How did you get to be an expert on romance? Walt Phillips?"

"As if. Romance novels."

"Books?"

"Books are a perfectly legitimate method for learning. That is why they use textbooks in school."

Now he had that image stuck in his head. VJ in a classroom wearing a school uniform and clutching a tattered paperback with a half-naked Viking on the cover. Naturally, that progressed to imagining VJ half-naked. The camera would love the color of her skin and capture the perfect lines of her body with a reverence he'd seldom experienced behind the lens.

"Go for it, then," he said. "I can't wait to learn about romance according to VJ."

"Well." She sat up in the seat, instantly animated. "Romance has stages. A progression. You can't dive right into bed."

Really. Who says? VJ might need an education of her own.

With that thought, he forgot about the camera. This was his scene, and he'd maim anyone who tried to take him out of it. He was having fun. What was the harm in playing along? "Stage one. No diving into bed. Got it."

She shook her head. "That's not stage one. Be quiet and listen. The goal isn't to learn the stages. It's to understand them. Believe them. Recognize them as truth. So then it'll be obvious you're not in love with Kyla."

His eyebrows flew up. "That's the goal?"

Fantastic. He was already ahead. Never once had he mis-

taken what he felt for Kyla as love. Her talents were legend-
ary and he appreciated them—both on the screen and between
the sheets. But then, they'd drifted apart so long ago, he barely
even remembered the latter. Maybe it hadn't been all that spec-
tacular.

"Yeah," she said. "When we're through with all the stages,
you'll admit you're not in love with Kyla."

VJ's wholesomeness pricked at his sense of honor. How fair
was it to play this game when he had no illusions about his relationship with Kyla?

Love and marriage had little to do with each other and
neither had anything to do with him. This desert mirage had
about a point zero-zero-one percent chance of convincing him
differently.

"So, what if I admitted that right now?"

VJ off took her sunglasses and stared at him openly. "Clearly
you didn't understand the rules. I'm supposed to go through
the stages and *then* you admit it. Why in the world would you
marry Kyla if you're not in love with her?"

"I never said I was marrying her. I said I was announcing
our engagement. Let's not get ahead of ourselves."

"Oh, pardon me for assuming an engagement leads to a
wedding." She made a disgusted little noise. "That's your problem in a nutshell. You think these things are all separate and
they're not. You need romance instruction worse than anyone
I've ever met."

He couldn't stop the grin. "Then educate me."

"I'm not sure it'll help. You might be too far gone." She
licked her lips and faced forward. "Are you going to marry
her or not?"

"It's…" *Complicated.* When had that become the norm for
his life? "Look, I know I said to ask instead of assuming, but
this is the sole exception. I'm announcing our engagement,
and she's well aware that I'm not in love with her. Leave it at
that, okay?"

"Okay." She drawled out the syllables, overloading them with meaning.

Great. She'd taken him at his word and created all sorts of assumptions. Well, if he hadn't wanted that, he should have kept his mouth shut. But he hadn't. She deserved as much honesty as he could give her, and now it was time to drop it.

"So, what's stage one?"

For a beat, she didn't respond, like she'd changed her mind about educating him.

"Attraction." Her legs slid together and crossed, slowly, snagging his attention from the road. "A sense of awareness that wasn't there a minute ago. Maybe you've known each other for years and one day, something happens. Pop! You notice how nice her eyes are or how sexy she looks in that shirt. Maybe you're strangers, but eyes meet across a smoky room at a party and it's a lightning bolt to the spine."

Or an orange pickup pulls off the road and out spills a provocative sunflower with coconut-scented hair. "Hormones. Like I said."

"If you want to be clinical." She frowned and the shadow of a road sign threw her into murkiness, then rushed away. "Reality is much more complex. Why do your hormones react to this woman and not that woman? For example."

Interesting point. She wasn't spouting text from the pages of a bodice-ripper. Some analysis had gone into this. "Maybe that woman is a pain in the butt."

"We're still in the attraction stage. You wouldn't know anything about the woman's personality in a relationship at this point. That's the next stage. Once you recognize some primal, fundamental reaction to her, then comes stage two."

"Which is?"

"Attention."

Subtly, she shifted closer, and below his sleeve, a firm breast brushed his biceps. A breast only covered by a thin shirt and definitely not encased in a bra.

"You pay attention to her," she said. "Not like giving her lame flowers from Piggly Wiggly. But paying attention to stuff she likes. Music. Books she's read. You notice little variations in the color of her skin. You give her a nickname. Remember details, like the things she says." Her breast nudged his arm muscle with little licks of heat. "Stage one and two. You're hot for her, and you pay attention."

Hot. Yeah. His lungs were on fire with the effort it took not to gulp oxygen. He was swamped in the sensation of a rough cotton T-shirt against his arm, the only barrier between his skin and hers, and it was a miracle the zipper on his jeans hadn't busted a few teeth.

"How many stages are there?" he asked, his voice involuntarily husky.

"Six," she said and her voice had dipped a couple of notches, too, causing her answer to sound like *sex*. Or maybe that was due to his hormone-laced senses. "Romance isn't simple."

What was simple? Not this blazing stage one between them, which had to be leaving scorch marks on her, too, as perceptive as she was. Besides, she might have been serious enough with a guy to be talking marriage, but that didn't make her experienced.

Then there was the engagement, which had to be real to the public in order to work. He wasn't sure of Kyla's angle yet, but if the engagement was designed to throw them back together like he suspected, she'd perceive VJ as competition. No one deserved to be in those crosshairs.

He sighed. The reasons for nipping this thing with VJ in the bud were legion.

Because this situation didn't suck enough, he'd just transformed VJ into ripe, delicious, forbidden fruit. Cursing, he yanked on the wheel and swerved to avoid a dead armadillo.

Half-blind, he struggled to keep his attention on the road and off VJ.

Stop. Detach. Immediately.

He hated to step on any of her puppies, let alone her fanciful ideas about romance. Unfortunately, it might be the only solution capable of getting his mind out of the gutter.

"This is all fascinating. But I don't believe in fairy tales."

"Who said anything about fairy tales?" VJ countered and wiped damp palms on her jeans stealthily, so Kris remained unaware of how nerves were kicking her butt. "Romance instruction" had grown from a ploy to prove he wasn't in love with Kyla, which he'd readily admitted, into a death match of wills over something far worse. He didn't believe in romance. And she was going to change his mind.

"Romance novels are not fairy tales. I'm talking about real life."

"Whose real life? Yours?"

"Sure. One day." She shrugged. "That's why I said no to the proposal. Walt Phillips and romance don't even speak the same language. It might as well be Greek."

She winced. Freudian slip. Or something. This conversation was going to kill her one way or another.

With a hint of a smile, Kris peeked over the rim of his sunglasses and said something foreign and sexy. "I'll translate that for you some other time."

Her breast still tingled where it had touched his arm and that voice did nothing but heighten it. What was she doing? Was this really about changing his views toward romance or a thinly veiled excuse to get close to him now that she knew his relationship with Kyla was not what it seemed?

The car passed the Van Horn city limit. "Okay, now I'm hungry," she said, even though she wasn't. She needed time to regroup. "We can stop here for breakfast."

Kris pulled into a crowded fast-food place without comment.

He parked the Ferrari among rusted flatbeds, semis and beat-up four-doors, then sped around to her side to help her out of the low seat. Always a gentleman, and jumping jellybeans was that ever attractive. She took his hand, and the contact sparked. "Would you mind ordering? I want to freshen up."

He nodded and followed her inside, where she fled to the filthy bathroom. The crust on the sink lost her attention when she caught sight of the dark welt under her eye. No wonder he'd freaked. She looked horrific.

Kris didn't believe in fairy tales because his entire life already was one. She had to believe in them. Otherwise, how could she possibly hold out hope that life might be different than the tragedy she'd escaped?

They ate breakfast in silence, or rather, he ate and she picked at her sausage. The longer they didn't talk, the tighter the tension stretched, and it wasn't helped by the fact that watching him do anything with his hands set off a throb low in her belly.

"Can I borrow your phone?" she asked when he stood to collect trash from the table.

"Sure. It's in the car."

"Do you mind giving me some privacy?" She jerked her head in the direction of the Ferrari. "I have to let someone know I'm okay. I'll just be a minute."

Without a word, he slid his gorgeous body back into the molded chair with grace, which made *not* imagining those long, golden limbs wrapped around hers impossible.

"Let me know when it's safe," he said.

She bit back a snort. "You haven't figured it out yet? You'll never be safe from me." Then she spun on a toe and flounced to the car, heart pounding in her throat as she elbowed through the throng of testosterone checking out Kris's Ferrari.

She should be committed. Romance instruction. Where did she come up with these ideas? The best plan was to focus on getting to Dallas and then, the rest of her life. Kris had no place in the middle of that, even without the nebulous engagement. He was from Hollywood. She wasn't.

His phone lay in the hollow between their seats. *The* seats.

Nothing in the car belonged to her except her bag. She had to remember that.

After three fumbles with the confusing little pictures crowding the screen of Kris's phone, she figured out how to play a fishing game, use the timer and search for a restaurant on Santa Monica Boulevard. Then she found the section that looked like numbers to dial an honest phone call. Rich people.

She shook her head as Pamela Sue said hello on her end.

"It's me."

"VJ. Thank God." Pamela Sue heaved out a long sigh. "Your daddy's been here twice, saying you've been gone since last night."

The hot leather burned into her thighs as she shifted to find a more comfortable spot. "I'm okay. I'm on my way to Dallas."

"Dallas? How'd you get to the bus station? No one's been near Van Horn—"

"I'm with Kris."

"*Kris?* Kristian Demetrious? That Kris? Wait. Are you with Kris, or *with* Kris? Hold on, let me sit down." Bedsprings squeaked in the background. "In case it's better than I'm imagining."

"Don't be ridiculous," VJ hissed and darted a glance through the tinted window to make sure that Kris wasn't strolling across the concrete toward the car. "It's not like that. He's surrounded by beautiful women all the time. He doesn't have to pick up waitresses along the road."

"Hey, you were Miss Little Crooked Creek a couple of times. You're every bit as beautiful as they are," Pamela Sue insisted. "Don't sell yourself short."

She smiled a little at the blind loyalty. Pamela Sue hadn't seen her face and therefore didn't realize VJ resembled a raccoon. "I love you, even when you're lying."

"Well, I hate you. A lot. How dare you ride off into the sunset with a sexy guy in a sexy car? I'll never forgive you unless you have a smoking hot affair and spill every last detail."

"Deal." She sobered. "Don't tell anyone, okay? It's a secret. The media, you know."

She didn't think Daddy would come after her all the way to Dallas, but it couldn't hurt to take precautions.

"Oh, yeah. I do know. The media chases me around all the time." Pamela Sue cleared her throat. "What happened, VJ? I know you didn't hop on the first set of testicles to wheel through town. This isn't like you."

"Nothing happened. It was time." She injected a note of levity. "I ran into Kris this morning, and he offered me a ride. How could I refuse? Long way to Dallas. Lots of opportunity to help him forget about those beautiful women he used to know."

Pamela Sue laughed and a tear slipped down VJ's cheek. They'd never lied to each other. Never. But neither would she let anyone think of her as a victim, besides Kris, but only because it was too late. Pamela Sue might run straight to Bobby Junior or Tackle, tattling about how VJ had been hit. There was a part of her that wondered if they'd let Daddy slide or take his side out of loyalty. If she lost that battle, what then? She'd rather take the real rescue from her knight in a shining Ferrari.

"You gonna stay with Jenny Porter's cousin?" Pamela Sue asked.

"Yeah." Beverly Porter wouldn't mind if VJ asked to stay on her couch until the condo was finished. The worst thing that could happen is she'd have to pay rent early. Or at least that's what she kept telling herself.

"Call me when you get to Dallas. Be careful."

"Yes, ma'am. No talking to strangers."

"I meant buy a box of condoms."

A diluted laugh slipped out and was ragged enough to communicate to her best friend what she couldn't say aloud. "Good bye, Pamela Sue."

She hung up—or at least she thought she did after punching random pictures on the slick screen—and went to retrieve her Greek god.

When she rushed back into the main dining room, Kris was staring at the flaking wall, chiseled lips pursed and troubled, fingers drumming the table.

"Ready?" he said, and unfolded his frame from the chair-table combination bolted to the floor.

Something was off in his rigid stance. An invisible layer drenched with stress. "What's wrong?"

"I'm ready to go. After you." His granite expression didn't waver, reminding her of inaccessible Kristian Demetrious from the diner when he'd faced down her brothers.

This time, that look was directed at her. Their interaction was a lot of things, most of it too difficult to pin down, but she couldn't stand for *strained* to be on the list. The foreign engine in his mind had begun to reveal its secrets, and she wanted to take it apart to see what made it tick.

She let it drop until they'd both slid into their seats and he hit the button to start the engine. Over the hefty roar, she said, "If you want to talk, I'd be happy to listen."

"I said there's nothing wrong."

"No," she said. "You said you were ready to go, as if to imply you were impatiently waiting for me. You're restless, not impatient."

His expression relaxed. "I've got a lot of things on my mind."

"Of course you do." Impulsively, she threaded his golden fingers through hers. After a not-so-quick squeeze, she let go. "Being responsible for an entire movie must be a heavy burden."

His forehead scrunched. "It is. Most people don't get that. But I don't think of it that way."

"How do you think about it?"

As they sat in the parked car, the air conditioner blasted to life, jetting dark strands of hair off his cheekbones. "Blank canvas. I have this story in my head and a million frames to capture it. Until the final cut, it can turn into anything I choose. There's a lot of power in committing my vision to permanency.

And a lot of nail-biting because I'm opening it to be interpreted through someone else's lens."

The tension had almost totally drained away. "What's the first step when you start a film? Wait." Before her burst of daring fled, she reached over and slipped off his sunglasses. "Now talk. Your eyes do this thing when you're passionate about the subject, and I want to see it."

He swiveled his head to capture her gaze, and her diaphragm seized so hard, she went light-headed. A baptism of liquid fire washed over her skin as his hard brown eyes roamed across her face.

"What do they do?" he asked and she would have sworn he didn't move, but suddenly, they were a breath apart. About to kiss.

"What does what do?" she whispered, afraid to shift, afraid to exhale, afraid to think.

"My eyes. When I'm talking about a film. What happens?"

"Oh. Um." Simple language escaped her. All she could concentrate on was the fiery, clamping need twisting through her abdomen. She ached to lean into the space between them, to lose all sense of time in the raw pressure of his lips on hers.

That mystical connection beckoned, laden with promise.

A car horn startled her and she jerked. Backward, not forward, breaking her gaze. She scrambled to pick up the threads of conversation. "Um, they light up. Your skin holds everything inside but the passion builds and builds and the only place it can escape is through your eyes."

He shifted smoothly, drove out of the parking lot and merged onto the freeway. Obviously unaffected. She'd overreacted to the almost kiss. That, or he spent his day fending off forward women and took it in stride.

His face implacable now, he said, "You have an active imagination. I approach film as an art, but it's also critical to stay detached. Too much emotional investment leads to sloppy structure."

"Nice try. But you can't will it away, Lord Ravenwood."

"I'm sorry, what?"

"Lord Ravenwood," she said with an airy wave. "He's the duke in *Embrace the Rogue,* the finest book about romance ever written. He hides from his emotions, too."

"Really." Sarcasm oozed from his clipped response. "That's what you think I do? Hide?"

"Yeah. I bought your line about not believing in fairy tales, but I see now that it's not true. That's not your actual problem." The angel on her shoulder screamed at her to shut up. This couldn't lead to anything other than disappointment and grief when he went back to Hollywood. But he was lying to himself. She couldn't sit idly by while he coasted through life, completely isolated, when it was obvious he yearned to cross that chasm with the gas pedal to the floorboard.

"Since you've got me all figured out, what's my actual problem?"

This amazingly sensual man seemed content with a bloodless Hollywood-style engagement to someone he didn't love, and, if she'd correctly interpreted his careful response, had no intention of marrying—all to secure the right backers for his film.

He needed to be shown what a mistake he was about to make. He needed VJ to set him free from his self-imposed prison. If he'd given any indication of having a real relationship with Kyla, she'd have backed off. But he'd done the exact opposite. Deliberately, she was convinced.

"You want desperately to believe. You're just too afraid."

The devil on her other shoulder whispered, *Time for stage three.*

Five

Perfect. Instead of carefully steering around VJ's fanciful ideas, he'd driven her to psychoanalyze him. Incorrectly.

Kris laughed, but it sounded hollow. "I'm not afraid of fiction. That's why I'm a filmmaker, to create fictional worlds. But fiction is not reality. Real life's tough. You get knocked down a lot and each time, it's harder to pick yourself up."

The dark shadow across VJ's cheek taunted him from his peripheral vision. Of course she knew the realities of life and didn't need to be preached to about them.

VJ was a rare woman, determined to reach for her destiny instead of waiting around for it to find her. He admired that.

And, she'd easily pulled him out of his bout of brooding. Some of Kyla's best off-screen performances included temper tantrums about his moods. VJ was a force to be reckoned with.

"You're absolutely right," she said. "Do you think we'll reach Dallas by dinnertime?"

"Why? You got a hot date?"

She meticulously inspected the rocky terrain out the passenger window. "You asking?"

"No," he said in a rush. He cleared his throat. "Maybe we'll grab dinner."

The truth was he liked her company. He liked the spike through the gut when her sizzling gaze caught him just right. She saw things, stuff no one else saw. Dangerous, all the way around, and he liked that, too.

It was a miracle he'd kept his hands off her this long, but he had to. And they still had a long, long way to go.

"Drive slower and we'll be having dinner together by default," she suggested, then threw in, "Maybe breakfast, too." Since his blood pressure hadn't climbed high enough already.

Visions of a cozy, roadside motel spun through his head, where a convenient convention had booked all the rooms but one and they had no choice but to take the room with the solitary bed. Then… He groaned. Well, he'd been accused of a lot of things, but lack of imagination wasn't one of them. Lack of interest, yeah. Lack of attachment, definitely. Lack of emotion, without fail.

Before registering the impulse to do so, he'd backed off the accelerator. "I'm not in that big of a hurry."

"At that rate, you'll be driving backward before too long. I have a better idea. Take the next exit." She nodded at the green sign for a town called Lively.

Curious now, he gunned the Ferrari down the ramp and followed her directions to the center of town. Such as it was. The rustic buildings, peeling paint and layer of dust were markedly similar to the rut in the desert VJ called home.

At the end of Main Street, she pointed left and he turned into the middle of a traveling carnival set up in the parking lot of the local grocery store. Flashing lights on the large Ferris wheel winked in the midmorning sun and music piped from hidden speakers. Cheerfully painted booths promising big prizes lined the parking lot.

A carnival. Really.

"It'll be fun, I promise." VJ grinned mischievously. "And, it's the ideal place for you to learn about stage three."

"Romance instruction at a carnival?" He slid out of the car and went around.

He'd been praying romance instruction had been forgotten because he had a sneaking suspicion about the direction it was headed, and stomping caution flat seemed like the opposite of a good idea.

"Yes, definitely," she said as he took her hand to help her out of the car.

He followed her to the nearest blood-red ticket booth and fished out his wallet to hand over enough cash to last for hours. Or at least long enough to find out what stage three was. Whichever came first.

Kris ushered VJ into the den of iniquity she'd chosen as the means to educate him on the fine points of romance. Or was it love? With VJ, it seemed they were one and the same.

"We've beaten the crowd," Kris commented as they strolled the deserted midway. VJ's gaze flitted everywhere at once and he smiled, oddly charmed. The awe on her face was worth the price of admission. "Are you in the mood for rides or games?"

"The Scrambler."

This obviously wasn't her first carnival. "Which one is that?"

She pointed. At the other end of the midway, the ride spun drunkenly, a smudge of red, green and yellow against the backdrop of mountains and sky. Wonderful. One of those toss-your-cookies-at-the-end rides. She sauntered off and he hurried to catch up.

She was being unusually closemouthed. His curiosity was killing him. What was stage three?

In anticipation of her explanation, his senses honed in on the smallest detail. The swish of her jeans as she walked, thigh against thigh. The precise point at which the T-shirt dipped against the creamy hollow of her throat. He was getting a head-ache from sidelong glances at the riot of colors corkscrewing through her curls from crown to tip. Some auburn, thin blond streaks and that warm cinnamon. He wanted to slide a strand against his palm—to test the temperature.

His fingers clenched into a fist against his leg.

Her hand accidentally bumped his and the spot on his knuckle where they'd touched turned immediately sensitive. Her heat was blatant, easy to sort from the radiating concrete, but not easy to dismiss.

He was obsessing over the way VJ walked. What was wrong with him? He'd spent less time setting up a camera to shoot a Dutch angle.

An agonizingly silent eternity later, he followed her into the Scrambler's empty queue. They threaded through the turns and at the bend of one, he misjudged her speed. The collision of his chest with her back triggered a shock. He got a whiff of coconut from her hair and blood shot straight to his groin.

Torture. That must be stage three. There was no other ex-planation.

A grizzled ride operator took the tickets from Kris's hand and lifted the bar on the closest car. Kris climbed in. VJ wedged in next to him, ignoring the four feet of seat on her other side. The operator slammed the bar into place, and as they were the only thrill-seekers around, shuffled off to the control box.

"Put your arm around me," VJ said, and nudged him when he didn't immediately comply. "I mean it. The centrifugal force on this thing is going to hurt if you don't."

Physics. That was a new angle. He secured his sunglasses, slung an arm around her shoulders, and she snuggled up against him, curving into his body naturally. Of course, because it fit well with the torture theme playing out under the guise of teaching him about romance.

Gears ground, tinny, harpsichord music bleated through the air, and the ride started spinning. As it gained momentum,

VJ pressed closer and closer until he couldn't have shoved her away with both hands, mostly because one was occupied with hanging on and the other had snaked into place against VJ's stomach, which filled his palm nicely. He thoroughly enjoyed it.

As he guessed was the intent.

Most of his blood kept his jeans uncomfortably tight, but some of it still circulated in his brain. Enough to be suspicious of the convenient ride choice.

Eventually, the ride slowed but his head kept going. The ride operator unlocked the safety bar, and Kris tried to stand, but his legs buckled. VJ was having trouble with watery legs, too, so he left his arm around her—to keep them both off the ground, no other reason. They staggered for the exit.

She led him to a couple of other rides in the same vein but he couldn't have named them at gunpoint. He was too busy inventing ways to continue innocently touching her. Taking her hand to help her into a ride. Brushing hair off her shoulder so it wouldn't get in her eyes when the speed increased. Buying a tub of buttery popcorn and reaching into it at the same moment she did.

It was challenging to keep rationalizing it as carnival fun, but she'd started it and he ached to finish it.

"Next up?" he asked. "Funnel cakes maybe?"

"Ferris wheel," she said decisively.

Abandoning pretense, he laced his fingers with hers and they ambled toward the Ferris wheel. She pretended not to notice they were holding hands, as if they'd done this a thousand times, but there was no way she could ignore the sizzle of awareness melding with the sun's heat. Thirst lashed the back of his throat, and the crevice between his shoulder blades beaded with sweat and frustration.

He was human and a guy. He needed water and VJ naked. Not necessarily in that order. Or separately. And he couldn't have the one he really wanted. Which sucked.

The Ferris wheel car swung dizzily as they settled into it,

or maybe his head was spinning with images of undressing VJ, slowly revealing those perfect breasts. Once the bar was secured, she turned and searched his face. Her eyes matched the summer sky, and it was the perfect shot. When was the last time he'd even thought about filming her? Forever ago, before the torture began. Before she'd dragged him under the hot spotlight of her gaze.

"So stage three." Her tongue darted out to moisten her lips. "Touching."

She trailed fingers along his arm, igniting landmines. The tips of her nails disappeared under his sleeve, just the tips, but it was so much sexier than if she'd gone straight for his zipper. The wheel turned, and he couldn't tear his eyes from hers.

"Touching," she repeated, her voice low. "Accidentally at first. Then you do it deliberately, because you can't unring that bell. Once you've got the imprint of her on your fingertips, it's like an addiction. You can't stop. You're thinking about the next hit before the current one's even faded."

Yeah, like imagining her forbidden fruit bared before him, his mouth open and all but salivating to taste her. He shut his eyes until the throb in his gut lessened enough to hopefully avoid an embarrassing accident.

"That's stage three. How'm I doing?"

His lids flew open. "Not bad. I wasn't expecting a demonstration along with the commentary."

Not bad? VJ was an evil genius.

"Demonstration?" she questioned primly. "I'm just having fun. Aren't you?"

"Oh, yeah, loads. This is the most fun I've had in ages." Actually, he was having fun in a perverse way. Nothing was going to happen with VJ—nothing he couldn't handle anyway.

They stopped at the zenith of the Ferris wheel. The vista was stunning—mountains, heat shimmers, vast blue…and VJ. Without thinking, he said, "Here's a romantic proposal spot."

She glared at him. "Are you making fun of me?"

"Not at all." Since their earlier conversation, the perfect proposal had been brewing in the back of his mind. He'd directed one in his third movie, and the scene had been flat. Faulty acting, he'd assumed. "But seriously. No guy spends more than five minutes on how to propose. She's going to say yes or no regardless of how you ask, right?"

"Do you practice being that cynical or does it come naturally?"

"Both. Come on." He nudged her with his elbow. "You know I'm right. If you were really, really in love with a guy and he got down on one knee in your living room after dinner, would you refuse because he asked without fanfare?"

"I don't know. I've never been really, really in love. Have you?" she asked, arms crossed and a defiant sparkle flushing her cheeks. God, she was beautiful.

"Hold on. You've never been in love but you're presuming to teach me about it?"

"Wow. The master of deflection, that's you. I'm not presuming to teach you anything. I *am* teaching you." She nodded to his hand, which rested unobtrusively, comfortably, on her knee. "Wasn't your last movie called *Twilight Murders?*"

"So?"

"How many murders have you committed, Mr. Big Shot Director?"

The grin cracked before he could check it. "You're amazing. Will you have my children?"

Frozen, she stared at him. "Do you take any of this seriously or am I wasting my time?"

"I don't know." He shrugged and set the car in motion. "What are you trying to accomplish? We blew past simple education a long time ago. What's the real goal here?"

She inspected the chipped paint on the safety bar, flicking off a small bit before answering. "To prove you suppress your passionate side."

He laughed. "You're going to fail miserably at that before

you even start. You've got me cast in your head as the real-world equivalent of your Duke Whoeverwood, but I'm just Kris. A guy who wants to make movies."

The catch in his throat shouldn't be there. He shouldn't have the urge to tell her she was right, or how so much of his soul ended up on the screen because it was the only place he could express himself without fear of turning into something monstrous. Like his father. "What you see is what you get. I'm not hiding or suppressing anything."

"You've got so much pent-up, seething passion inside, you can barely sit still."

"That's the sway of gravity against this monstrous Ferris wheel, babe." He crossed his arms to keep his hands where they belonged—off her.

Her teeth gleamed when she bared them. "And I disagree. Strongly."

Man, she pushed his buttons. Every single one. What was he supposed to do with her? What *could* he do?

Nothing.

The film was too important to jeopardize over an alluring mirage, no matter how concrete she became.

Her eyelids drifted closed and then opened in a slow blink. Instantly, the atmosphere turned sensual. She studied him, an allover perusal loaded with hot appreciation. "This shirt is soaked."

She bunched the cotton up between her breasts, baring her midriff, and with the other hand, fanned her face. That swatch of glistening skin below her shirt drew his eye magnetically. The tiniest sliver of the underside of her breast peeked out from the cotton.

He hardened in an instant. Did she have a clue what she was doing?

"Seems like we've been stuck here for an hour," he said hoarsely in an attempt to dial down the heat. "Wonder why we're not moving?"

"I paid the operator to take a break once we got to the top," she said. "You didn't notice. It'll be a while till we're on the ground. So here we are, me and you. And no prying eyes."

"Why'd you do that?"

She pierced him again with her know-all, see-all gaze. "The view."

"You're not even looking at it."

"Yeah, Kristian, I am."

His name rolled off her tongue like molasses-coated barbed wire. Except for the media, nobody called him Kristian. And nobody ever would again, not like that. He yearned to sink into her and never come up for air.

With one finger, she swept a thatch of hair behind his ear, and the light touch curled his toes. She threaded strands through her fingers, letting it waterfall away, and exhaled in a raspy moan that speared his hard-on. That had to be the sexiest sound ever.

Deep in her throat, she moaned again. "I want you to kiss me. Do you know how bad I want it?"

At least as badly as he wanted to. He tried to think about something unsexy. Not happening.

"I have a pretty good idea," he muttered.

One hot hand wandered over his chest, delving into the dips of his muscles and tracing the line of his collarbone. Pushing him toward insanity. He wished she'd find the hem, slide underneath the T-shirt. Touch his bare skin and say his name again.

"I'm dying for you to kiss me," she said. "But you can't. We can't."

Can't? Says who?

He shook his head, hard. No, it was true. They couldn't.

Then she leaned in with the smallest incline of her head, offering up lips puckered in a superb *O*. Just before she hit the point of no return, she whispered, "Kristian."

Her breath brushed his jaw, swirled down his throat and spread through his body, heating it, warming corners he'd have insisted weren't cold. The space between them slowly disappeared. Too slowly.

His control vanished. He shoved fingers through her hair, cupped the back of her head and kissed her. Hard. Open-mouthed. Tongue seeking, sliding along hers in a fiery path. Tasting every crevice of her smart mouth. Unleashing the frustration he couldn't ease any other way.

At last.

He dragged her half into his lap and worked a hand under her shirt to thumb one of those taut nipples. Perfection. One should be in his mouth. Right now. He growled.

More.

He changed the angle and drew her tongue deeper into his mouth, sucking on it with quick little pulls then broke away to bite his way down her neck, back up to her earlobe. He took it in his mouth and nibbled on the sweet flesh.

He needed more.

Her hot lips locked onto his. Hot, so hot. He guided her hand to his groin and dragged her palm across the rock-hard bulge, nearly exploding right then and there from her blistering touch.

With a lurch, the Ferris wheel started up again and jolted them apart. Bleary-eyed, he fought through the lust-induced haze, taking in VJ's mussed hair and swollen lips both screaming *take me fast.* He barely resisted yanking her back.

"Good thing you're so, um, reserved," she said without a trace of irony, her irises molten and seductive. "That was so tame, I invited the Baptist Knitting Club over to watch."

A good, honest laugh burst out in spite of it all, and he winced as vibrations traveled through his throbbing erection. He'd never had a chance. Hadn't wanted one. "Okay. You made your point."

And how.

It was disturbing how easily she'd snapped his control and how much he'd liked letting go into that dark free fall of passion. Disturbing how accurately she'd gauged the truth. Disturbing and unprecedented.

"Kissing is stage four," she said. "By the way."

Of course it was. A sin and a shame he liked her so much because only the worst kind of slime could pretend to be engaged to Kyla while having an extremely satisfying side-thing with VJ. That wasn't fair or respectful to either woman.

No, VJ was the marrying sort of woman. He knew that. Now that his brain was functioning—the real one, not the one he'd been using five seconds ago—he had to face that he'd crossed so far over the line, it was but a distant slash.

It couldn't happen again. He probably wouldn't be able to look in the mirror as it was. No matter how much he burned to dive into the pleasure VJ promised, he had to stay in control from now on. It was totally not cool to lose it like that. He kept himself in check for a reason, usually without any trouble. VJ was exceptionally unique in more ways than one.

And he was still so hard, he couldn't walk.

While Kris took a moment in the portable bathroom, VJ slumped on a bench with a great view of the Ferris wheel and fingered her chafed lips.

The vilest word she'd ever said aloud slipped out. She clapped a hand over her mouth. Mama was surely rolling over in her grave. Her daughter was nothing but a cursing harlot. The only thing VJ had proven at the top of the Ferris wheel was that a small-town girl like her couldn't handle the highly specialized, foreign engine beneath the hood of Kristian Demetrious.

Kissing him had been like licking a nine-volt battery. A stun to the tongue and ill-advised.

A man who could kiss like that, and likely had many other talents, chewed up women and spit them out on a regular basis. She'd set him free, all right. Naively, she'd assumed her vast understanding of men in books would transition to men in real life and the truth put a huge chink in her delusions.

She was so out of her league.

Kris came into view, his gait easy and loose and sexy. Ebony, glossy hair brushed his shoulders. Good night, the man was hot. There'd been a possibility the chemistry between them would disappear after her stage-four experiment. The exact opposite was what had happened. And now she knew what his golden hands felt like when they touched her. Just watching him move made her squirm.

She was in so much trouble. People in Hollywood played at relationships, played at things she held dear, like long-term commitment. Kris had flat-out admitted as much, then she practically handed the man an engraved invitation for a one-night stand.

Was that really what she wanted?

"Ready?" she said and gave him an everything's-cool smile. Ferris wheel music crashed through the midway, loud and raucous.

He paused in front of her, crossed his arms and peered over the rim of his sunglasses. "Were you the slightest bit affected by that kiss or was it strictly designed to prove me wrong?"

Her mouth fell open. "I'm not quite that blasé about having the inside of my skin set on fire. But I'll take it as a compliment that you have to ask."

"Is that a yes?"

"Does it matter?"

"Yeah." He frowned. "Well, no. Not really. You and I both know the score here. Right?"

Nodding, she stifled the urge to scream at him to shut up and let her have her fantasy for a while longer. "Of course. I proved you suppress your passions, just like Lord Ravenwood, so I win."

He grinned, and her heart grew a little heavier. All the

inconvenience of her misinterpreting that kiss as something meaningful was alleviated.

She couldn't be too upset. This was her fault, after all, for leaping into deep water without a floaty.

But provoking Kris into boiling over had been too easy to resist. A man more in denial didn't exist.

"So," he said. "Does that mean I get to move on to stage five?"

"If you want to," she said nonchalantly, though this whole game of romance instruction had become a lot less fun now that she'd unlocked him. Every sinfully delicious bit of that stormy passion called to her, and she wanted badly to answer.

But not badly enough to let him love her and leave her. "I figured we were done since I proved my point."

Something sizzled through his expression, but with the dark shield of his sunglasses in place, she couldn't interpret it. She'd rather he hadn't put them back on.

"Not by half," he said.

Pain stabbed at the backs of her eyes. So he wanted to play, as long as she didn't read too much into it. Was she completely crazy to consider it?

Yes. She *was* crazy. Except she *knew* he'd been trying to tell her something without telling her when he hinted the engagement wasn't exactly typical. He'd deflected the question about whether he'd ever been in love far too fast. His heart was buried underneath layers of cynicism and Hollywood.

What if she could uncover it?

Oh, how she wanted to, wanted all of him. The taste of that untamed kiss still blasted the roof of her mouth. If she had any hope of moving past flirtation, any hope of guiding him away from the weird engagement, any hope of claiming all that passion for her very own, stage five was the key.

"Then we better get started." She grasped his proffered hand. "Stage five is very tricky."

Six

The interior of the Ferrari was the perfect temperature to bake a cobbler in less than ten minutes, and the heat smacked VJ the moment she slid into the passenger seat. "Hurry with the air conditioner."

Kris dropped into his seat and hit the ignition. The sun wasn't the only thing heating up the interior. But it was the one she could reasonably handle at the moment. Cool air washed over her as he drove out of Lively and onto the freeway toward Dallas.

"Music?" he asked.

"Not the sexy stuff. Something else." She couldn't take the thrum of Spanish guitars right now. Here in this exotic, European car, surrounded by unimaginable luxury and privilege intrinsic to people in Kris's stratosphere, her resolve didn't feel so...resolved.

An upbeat tune sailed out of the speakers, and he immediately turned it down so it was atmospheric background noise.

"So, stage five," she said. "It's emotion."

"I was hoping it was sex."

Of course he was. No surprise after she threw herself at him on the Ferris wheel.

Sex echoed in her mind and triggered visions of what might have happened if the Ferris wheel hadn't rotated at the very worst time.

Best time. *Best time.*

"That's because you're thinking like a guy."

"Yeah. I'm sort of bound by the equipment God gave me."

"That's why I'm here. To help you think with something other than your equipment."

His laugh crossed her eyes. There was something really powerful about making a man like Kris laugh. Especially because it was all she had to keep her warm at night, when it came down to it.

She could pretend all day long that stage five was the key, but in reality, unsophisticated VJ Lewis might need a million stages to crack Kristian Demetrious. She had about the same ability to decipher his instruction manual as she did the one for his car. Zero.

"I'll keep that in mind. So, emotion?"

The mere word hadn't scared him off the subject. But he wasn't most men, despite her intimate knowledge of his similar equipment. Her cheeks heated and she looked out the window so Kris didn't notice.

"Yep," she said to the glass, and her fingers curled into thin air of their own accord. She'd touched him. *There.* Her tummy flipped. He'd been harder than Texas soil in a drought. For her. No instruction manual needed to understand that. "Stage five. Figuring out her emotional needs and granting them."

"Just hers? Guys don't have emotional needs?"

"You're the one with the equipment. You tell me."

"Sure. We have a really emotional need to have as much sex as possible before we die. Survival of the species, you know."

"Yeah. Survival." She rolled her eyes because it seemed

like an appropriate reaction when two people shared a dangerous, seductive attraction and one of them felt totally out of her depth. "So that's why this is about her needs, because guys are easy."

"It might be easy to get us willing, but that's not what we're talking about, is it? This is all about romance. I'd love to know a woman's secret for romancing a guy."

So would she. Especially the one in the next seat. Then maybe stage five wouldn't feel so insurmountable.

She shook her head. "No way, Jose. Women everywhere would throw rotten tomatoes at me as I passed by on the street if I told you."

He snapped his fingers in mock disappointment. "Fine, then. Tell me what I'm supposed to be doing to figure out her emotional needs."

"That was the paying attention stage. You should already know. Now you have to do it."

For a minute, he was quiet, as if processing, and the steady hum of tires on concrete filled the car. "So I've figured out what her greatest emotional need is and I've done it. What do I get out of the deal?"

His sidelong glance caught her in the abdomen. A lock of hair fell against his cheekbone. His hair was unbelievably glossy and soft and now that she knew what it felt like, it was so much harder not to touch.

She sat on her hands. "You're hopeless. I thought we'd made more progress. You get the realization you're in love and it's going to last forever. Stage five means you're thinking about someone else instead of your own selfish needs. That's the definition of love. Sacrificing what you want to make someone else happy."

"And in your mind, romance and love are the same."

"They're not in yours?"

Instantly, his expression iced over, and the chill infused her skin. "Not at all," he said. "Love is elusive. Fleeting. It doesn't last, and therefore it's too difficult to pin down with a simple definition. Romance is all about action. A back and forth. Doing something to get somewhere."

"Nice." She tsked to clear the tremor in her throat. He was speaking from the rock bottom of his shriveled heart, and nothing she'd said was getting through. "So, it's all a necessary evil to get a girl naked."

"That's not what I meant." His frustrated growl coaxed a smile from her. "Romance is a verb. There's a physical aspect you can point to and say there's the romance in this scenario. Like flowers. The right lighting, the setting."

"Flower is a noun, Kris. And love is more of a verb than romance. You can't say 'I romance you.' Well, I guess you can, but you'll sound like English is your second language."

"English *is* my second language."

He glared at her, and she started giggling uncontrollably. "I'm sorry. I'm picturing you swooning at my feet as you declare, 'I romance you.'"

She laughed so hard, she couldn't stop, and had to wipe tears from her eyes, ignoring the couple extra that squeezed out. That was stupid, to cry over the fact that such a passionate, expressive man had been hurt badly enough to believe love didn't last. Yet she presumed to heal all that in a couple of hours. How big *was* her ego?

Kris's lips were twitching. "Glad you could find some amusement at my expense."

More giggles slipped out, and the tears threatened to spill over. "Sleepless night catching up to me. Sorry."

He captured her hand and kissed the back of it. Casually, like they were an old married couple—except the way his lips grazed her skin should come with a hazard warning. "Sleep, then," he said. "I'll let you argue with me about this later, since you're not going to win anyway."

She folded her still-sparking hand into her lap, all traces of humor dried up. "Okay. I am exhausted."

She faked a yawn, pillowed her arm against the door, then lay on it. When she closed her eyes, she swore she'd only think about football and what kind of job she'd get in Dallas. But the Ferris-wheel kiss drove all that out of her mind. Instead, she replayed it over and over and over, extending it in a torturous parade of images where Kris swept her away in a sensual haze and made love to her until dawn.

With a start, she woke and only then realized she'd fallen asleep. "What time is it?"

Kris glanced at the dash clock. "Almost two. Are you ready for lunch?"

"Yeah. I'd like to get out of the car for a while."

And prolong the inevitable. Dallas loomed at the edge of the horizon and she'd slept away a good bit of her precious few hours with Kris. In no time, they'd go their separate ways. Nothing had changed that, and nothing likely would—unless she came up with a heck of a Hail Mary.

They ate more fast food and talked. Kris told fascinating stories of growing up in Greece and spending his youth on his father's boats. She entertained him with anecdotes of redneck politics, of which she had an endless supply.

How in the world had Kris ended up so down-to-earth instead of obnoxious and stuck-up like all the rich people on TV? He'd grown up Trump wealthy, and after a painful fallout with his father, turned his back on the money and left Greece forever to follow his dreams of being a filmmaker, on his terms. She couldn't even find a way out of her pathetic life on her own.

No wonder she'd been thus far unable to pile-drive through the brick wall in his chest. She'd invented a crazy notion about saving him from a bloodless engagement to Kyla Monroe, one of the most successful and accomplished actresses in Hollywood.

But they were made for each other. Even if they weren't in love or getting married, at some point, they'd found a mutual appreciation and likely enjoyed common interests. A woman like Kyla didn't have to resort to flirting and stupid games like romance instruction to get Kris's attention. She already had it.

Somehow, VJ had convinced herself Kyla would be thrilled to get out of an engagement with someone who was only doing it for the sake of a film and it never occurred to her that the star of Kris's movie might be in it for the same reason.

Until now.

It was way past time to stop fantasizing about what could be and get some traction on the rest of her actual life.

"I need to borrow your phone again," she told him. "I'm sorry I have to be such a freeloader."

"VJ, I have an unlimited usage plan. You're not going to bankrupt me with two five-minute phone calls." He motioned to the Ferrari parked outside. "Help yourself."

"You're the only person on the planet who doesn't keep their phone on them." Even in Little Crooked Creek, ranchers dropped cell phones into the pockets of their jeans and teenagers texted each other as they walked to school.

He shrugged. "No one is so important they can't leave a message. Find me when you're done."

She slid into the Ferrari and dialed Beverly Porter on the first try. No one could say she didn't learn from her missteps.

Her only hope of shelter answered. "Beverly, it's VJ Lewis."

"Oh, hi. Just a minute." Beverly said something but it was muffled as if she'd put her hand over the speaker. "You're not calling to cancel on me are you? The condo's almost done."

Relief sang through VJ's veins. "The opposite, in fact. I'm on my way to Dallas and was hoping you wouldn't mind a roommate a little early."

She was pathetic, mooching off Beverly and barging into the one-person home of a girl she'd last seen over Fourth of July weekend last month. Friendship had its limits, and she was pushing them.

"Oh." Beverly's pause did not put VJ at ease. "You're on your way now? As in today?"

"I should be there by nine at the latest," VJ chirped, and winced at the fake brightness. "That's not too late, is it?"

"I'm really sorry, VJ. I'm in St. Louis at my grandparents' house. I had to let my old apartment go. They wanted me to sign another six-month lease or get out, and the condo won't be move-in ready for at least three weeks. My grandparents had an extra room and my boss is letting me work remotely. I had no idea you'd be moving so soon."

"No problem. I totally understand." There were bound to be loads of fifty-cent-a-night hotel rooms in Dallas.

"Do you have another place to stay?" Beverly's clear concern was almost her breaking point. "I know a few people who wouldn't mind."

Depending on the kindness of strangers. Even more pathetic. "That's okay. Thanks anyway. I'll find something else. I'll call you soon to give you my new phone number."

And that was that. Now she was homeless for the next three weeks.

VJ was eerily still for so long, Kris considered taking her temperature.

Each time the car passed another exit, he anticipated instructions to turn off so they could visit the world's largest ball of twine or the Petrified Wagon Wheel Museum, which VJ would artfully turn into a way to make him crazy. Or make him think. Or thaw him out a little more.

Each time she didn't speak, he grew more frustrated. He recognized the wisdom of taking big, giant steps back from that line. He did. He just didn't like it.

During the stage-five discussion, he'd had a hard time keeping his attention on the road and off her mouth. It wasn't only the things she said, but the way her lips formed the words, and how she never hesitated to spit out what was on her mind.

Twice, he'd had to physically restrain himself from pulling onto the shoulder in order to put that smart mouth to better use.

"You know what?" VJ said after several miles and several provocative images later of what those perfectly formed lips could do.

"What?"

"I turn twenty-five in two days, and I've never been outside of the state of Texas."

They'd have parted ways by then. He frowned at the sudden compulsion to stick around until her birthday and shower her with presents and champagne. "Do you want to go somewhere in particular or just over the state line?"

"I don't know. I haven't had the luxury of thinking about much more than the next dime in the bank. Mama was sick for so long and everything I planned to do..." She trailed off, and he had to swallow at the despondent note in her voice.

"Where would you go, right now, if money was no object?"

"Greece," she said instantly. "To see boats bobbing in crystal-blue water and watch the fishermen pull up nets. Like you talked about at lunch."

"Greece is nothing special. I couldn't leave fast enough." He'd walked out the door at sixteen and never looked back. Every once in a while, he missed odd things, like the strong tang of homemade *tsipouro*, which he used to drink with the help in the kitchen while Cook pretended not to notice. Strange—he'd lived in America now for the same length of time he'd lived in Greece. Sixteen years. Each place claimed half of his life, shaping him in different ways.

"Kris. I watched you talk about it. You can't pretend you don't miss it."

He downshifted, then couldn't figure out why he'd automatically gone for the gear shift when there was nobody in front of him.

No, that was a lie.

VJ unsettled him, and his response was to do something with his hands. Something other than touch her.

"I don't know what you think you see when I'm having a

regular, old conversation. My eyes are not the window to my soul," he said lightly.

"What is?"

"My films," he blurted out and then regretted it.

He opened his mouth to change the subject and suddenly didn't want to. Soon, he and VJ would arrive in Dallas and he'd never see her again. A margin of safety existed inside the car where real life didn't—couldn't—intrude. Her presence sharpened and clarified his thought process. His emotions. Why fight it? "No one else knows that."

"Because you hang out with all blind and deaf people?"

In spite of the somberness coating the back of his throat, he laughed. How did she do that? He had the capacity to fall into moodiness for days—had, many times—but she blew right through it as if it didn't exist. "Yeah. I guess so. But I don't sit around having heart-to-heart talks with anyone about why I love being a director, either."

"It'll be our secret, then." She smiled, and it dove right into his stomach. He forced his attention back to the road and tried to forget how her breast felt like velvet, which was impossible with the scent of coconut wafting in his direction as she leaned forward and said, "Tell me another one."

"I can't figure out the theme for *Visions of Black*." Wow, that had not been what he'd meant to say at all. "It's bothering me. Normally, I'd have all that down by now."

"What's the movie about?" Her hand inched closer to his but didn't touch it.

"It's a drama about a woman who wakes up in the hospital blind and suffering from amnesia, but she can see visions in her head of disjointed scenes. A persistence of vision she can't stop." He glanced at her, and she was watching him closely. No doubt picking apart his brain with her odd insight. "Persistence of vision is a theory that an image stays on the eye after that image has actually disappeared, which is how some scientists think people process the individual frames of film. So it all ties together. I'm boring you."

"Not at all," she said softly. "I love listening to you talk. Your voice does something to me. And it's kind of delicious."

The atmosphere in the car grew thick with thrumming anticipation again. He had to shift it, get a barrier up fast, or he was going to fall headlong into her and this time, he wouldn't stop. He cleared his throat. "The backing and publicity for *Visions of Black* are really important. My career is at stake. I've been trying for years to find the right combination of art and commercial success with no luck. In Hollywood, it's all about the numbers. A bigger budget and the right names attached to the movie are the only things I haven't tried." He fiddled with the air conditioner until it was blowing at exactly the same rate and temperature as before he'd started. "I have to do this, and Kyla's a big part of it. Film is important to me. It's my only outlet."

"Oh. I see."

He had a really distinct feeling she did. "No jokes about how repressed I am? You're not going to offer to be my other outlet? I handed that to you, gift-wrapped. With a bow."

She shrugged. "Trust me, I had a scintillating response on the tip of my tongue, but I'm going to apologize instead. I'm sorry I pushed you so hard. About love and romance. It's none of my business. I understand the engagement is important to the film. I'll back off."

The barrier thumped into place. Quiet filled the car and pressed down on his shoulders. "You don't have to apologize for having an opinion. A really strong opinion." She didn't smile. His shoulders got heavier. "Truthfully, I was looking forward to more stage five."

She sighed. "It's kind of pointless. You don't even believe in love."

Ouch. That pained expression on her face had him stumbling to speak. "What people think is love fades more easily than anyone will admit. Love is best confined to the screen, where it can last. So why not have a marriage based on a business agreement? At least then everyone's on the same page."

Even the idea of marriage nauseated him. Passion died, without a doubt, and when it did, a wife was on the front line for what it turned into. He couldn't allow that to happen to anyone, least of all to a person unfortunate enough to fall in love with him.

Passion didn't last. Love didn't last. His career had been built on capturing both the only possible way. The safest way.

"You're challenging me to prove love can last forever," she said. "Which is impossible since I haven't lived forever yet. Hook up with a vampire if you want better data."

"Until I find one, you're the only expert I've got. Why are you so sold on this whole idea of hearts and cupids? Read too many books?"

That was the wrong thing to say. Stiffly, she rested the side of her head on the glass, and he had the impression it wasn't far enough away for her. "I just am."

Something sharp clogged his windpipe. She had shut down, thanks to his stupid barriers, and he couldn't stand it. "You can't cop out. I'm being brutally honest. Now it's your turn."

She sank down in the seat. Way down. "I promised Mama. On her death bed."

The last word was cut off as she buried her face in the T-shirt's hem. Crying. Did his stupidity know no bounds?

Without hesitation, he took the next exit and rolled to a stop as soon as the car cleared the white line. Some things required his full attention. He stroked her back until she peered up from the pile of shirt. "Better now?" he asked.

"I'm not usually such a crybaby."

"I'm not usually such an idiot."

She choked out a laugh, and he finally took a deep enough breath to clear his head. One tear ran down her cheek and she seemed too drained to notice, so he wiped it away with the palm of his hand.

"I sat by Mama's bed and read to her," she said. His hand rested against her collarbone because he was unable to stop touching her while she hurt. "For two years. Romance novels because she liked knowing it was going to end happily. Mama had a tough life. She made me promise to find my own happiness outside of Little Crooked Creek, because she knew I'd end up like her if I stayed."

VJ's gaze sought and held his, begging him to understand. He did. The bruise under her eye said it all. Her hand slid up to cover his.

"I have to believe," she said. "Those stories aren't some author's imagination. The magic between a man and a woman is out there. All I have to do is find it."

"Magic?"

"Yeah, you know. The perfect blend of love, passion and friendship."

Agape, eros and *philia.* Magic was indeed the only way they'd ever come together in one person. He yanked his hand away. That was a whole boatload of puppies to step on and the poignancy behind her single-minded perseverance added a few kittens.

The fairy tale she sought wasn't some adolescent, misguided dream, it was a death-bed vow she intended to keep. She deserved a man who believed in the possibility of forever.

All the more reason to stay far, far removed from VJ. Emotionally and physically. Good thing they'd be parting ways soon.

"I hope you find it," he said sincerely. He liked the thought of her out there in the world, happy and fulfilled.

She searched his face, looking for something, and this time he wished he had it to give, but knew he didn't. The moment passed and he shrugged it off.

"Me, too," she said. "Though I need to find a place to stay

first. The condo I'm moving into won't be ready for three weeks and my roommate is out of town until then." She made a face. "So I'm homeless. Great plan on my part to escape Little Crooked Creek with no backup and no money."

"You don't have any money?" How did she intend to support herself? He'd assumed she had a place to go or they would have had this conversation before now.

Guarded tension hardened her expression. "I'll be okay."

"VJ." She wouldn't look at him. "You told me at the diner that you've been saving every dime. What happened to your money?"

"We have a long way to go. Get back on the freeway and drive."

"Like hell I will." This situation had him so angry he was cursing in English. "Answer the question."

She wrapped her arms around her chest like a shield. "I'm not your responsibility. I'll figure it out."

"In the dark? In a strange city? You have a screw loose if you think I'm going to let you fend for yourself. Keep your secrets about the money or don't. I don't care. But you're staying with me until you find other arrangements. Period."

Mouth tight, he stomped on the clutch, threw the car into gear and turned up the music so she couldn't argue. And so he couldn't hear his subconscious laughing at his pathetic effort to sound noble when he'd greedily latched on to this perfect excuse to keep her around.

"I'm not sharing a hotel room with you," VJ shouted over the music.

With a stab of his finger, he cut off the music. "I have a suite. Two bedrooms. So humor me," he said, keeping his eyes trained straight ahead. "And separate bathrooms before you start on that."

Like the insubstantial impediment of a wall mattered, when

VJ was on the other side of it, all gorgeous and amazing and alone.

How much of a glutton for punishment was he, really?

Seven

A modest square sign of carved ebony wood marked the entrance to Hotel Dragonfly, visually separating it from the short-circuiting neon signs of every motel in VJ's neck of the woods. Dallas really was in another realm.

Kris downshifted to turn into the drive and steered around a tour bus splashed with the name of a rap artist even VJ had heard of.

"Don't worry. He's one of the quieter ones." Kris nodded toward the bus resembling a giant bumblebee as he parked.

"I guess you know a lot of famous people." It wasn't a surprise, but she'd been enjoying her Ferrari bubble where no one existed except for her and Kris. "Have you stayed here before?"

"Several times. The Dallas Film Festival is where I won my first award and the Studios at Mustang Park are a Mecca for those of us in independent film." He helped her out of the car, and they walked to the lobby. "I'm going to use the studio for my new film, even though I'll have a larger budget. Kyla and I are supposed to meet with a couple of other people there on Tuesday."

That douse of cold water woke her up. She'd known he was driving to Dallas to meet Kyla, but it had always been later. Now it was now. "Is Kyla staying at this hotel, too?"

Lord have mercy, was she that daft? Of course Kyla was staying here. Probably in Kris's room. Just because they weren't getting married didn't mean they weren't sleeping together. She should have asked more questions a long, long time ago. She should have said no to the offer of a room.

As she weighed the mortification of sharing a hotel suite with the lovers versus another night on the street, he shook his head. "She's from Dallas. She's staying with her mom."

Breath she hadn't realized was trapped in her lungs hissed out. Kris and Kyla weren't involved. She'd stake her life on it. Regardless, he wasn't like that, looking for opportunities to humiliate her, and she was ashamed for even thinking it. He wanted to rescue her. Again. But without expecting anything in return. He was an all-around decent guy with hands skilled enough to make a girl lose her religion. A guy whom she did not have to say goodbye to for at least another night.

It didn't matter. *The Rescue of VJ Lewis* wasn't the title of a romance novel, and the extra room didn't mean anything other than a place to sleep. Space he thought nothing of offering because Kris was generous to a fault—as long as it didn't require him to give up anything emotionally important.

The chic clerk at the front desk greeted Kris by name, drew attention to her cleavage and dismissed VJ in one shot. VJ was too busy trying to hide the bruising on her face to have much energy left over to care. Kris slid a black credit card across the marble desk and smiled back at the tramp.

"How many keys, Mr. Demetrious?" Tramp asked.

"Two," he said and nodded to VJ. "Ms. Lewis is helping me with preproduction on my new film, and we have a lot of work to do."

"Of course," she said with a fake smile and tapped on the keyboard in front of her. She handed Kris a small envelope, carefully touching her fingers to his before releasing it. "Enjoy your stay."

VJ followed Kris to the elevator. Once inside, she glanced at him. "Smooth. Do you often squirrel away women in your hotel room under the guise of 'helping' with your movies?"

God on High, did she *really* want to know the answer?

Kris just laughed. "First time. Usually the hotel staff is pretty discrete. Have to be with so many headline-grabbers under one roof. But why invite someone to create a story where none exists?"

And didn't that bit of truth hit the barn broadside? Yep, no story here. He needed Kyla to make his movie, and VJ couldn't stand in the way. It meant too much to him. And she owed him an immeasurable debt. A step back from romance instruction and flirting and trying to claim his buried heart was the least she could do. Even if it made her eye sockets burn and her throat scratchy.

The top-floor suite defied description. She didn't want to touch anything lest the magic wear off. Espresso-stained modern furniture dotted the living area and splashes of sage green, beige and dark purple accented the uptown theme. There was a cozy dining-room table on a raised dais with a half circle of windows beyond it offering an unbroken view of downtown Dallas skyscrapers, all lit for the night in winking splendor. A small area with a sink, microwave and refrigerator occupied the space next to the table.

Small being relative. Her kitchen at home was half that size.

The last time she'd stayed in a hotel was the after-prom party, of which the remarkable highlights were Walt throwing up eight wine coolers on her dress and Pamela Sue helping clean it up in the tiny bathroom. This was…not even close.

As promised, two doors, one on each side of the room, led

to the bedrooms. "I'm going to sleep for about ten hours," she said.

"This one's yours." Kris guided her to the room on the left and opened the door. "Do you want dinner?"

"Not really. You've done enough for me already. I can't ever repay you."

She turned to enter the room so she could collapse but he stopped her with a solid grip on her arm. "VJ."

She kept her back to him.

Not now.

She might break into a million pieces if he said something sexy. Or nice. Or in Greek…

Actually, it didn't matter what he said, her fragileness was due to being at the threshold of the rest of her life and scared to death. Scared she couldn't hack life outside of Little Crooked Creek. Scared she'd made a mistake in getting into the Ferrari this morning. Scared she'd never find anyone else who lit her up inside like Kris did.

"Sleep well," he said and released her arm. She had the impression it wasn't what he'd intended to say but she didn't dare press it.

"Good night," she whispered and shut the door behind her.

The bedroom was done in the same style as the main area of the suite, but she hardly noticed it. She trudged to the giant, elegant bathroom and took off all her clothes. Her small bag looked forlorn and out of place against the richly tiled floor. Guests in a hotel like this probably had servants with more luggage. As if she'd needed some additional clues she didn't belong here.

A hot shower went a long way toward improving her mood. The boiler at home never gave up more than about ten minutes of hot water, and she loved every second of the half an hour she stood under the multiple jets and streams. Beautiful little bottles lining an indention in the shower wall contained exotically scented shampoo, conditioner and shower gel, which she gratefully used. Finally, she felt clean and stepped out, kicking her clothes under the vanity at the same time.

She dripped water all over the bathroom floor and spent longer mopping it up than she had energy for, but couldn't bear the idea of overworked maids cleaning up after her. In the drawer of the vanity, she found toothpaste, lotion and a brush and used them all.

Naked, she fell into the giant bed and wiggled under the covers.

When she woke, it was still dark. The clock on the chunky bedside table read 2:20 a.m.

Her stomach rumbled. It had been twelve hours since she'd eaten. She debated. Check the refrigerator in the other room for food or order room service? Either one would be charged to Kris's slick credit card.

She bit her lip. None of this was what she'd intended or expected. The lure of escaping with the gorgeous stranger in the *muy amarilla* Ferrari had been irresistible. An adventure with endless possibilities.

Well, here she was, smack in the middle of the only possible outcome. Gorgeous stranger was about to be engaged to Kyla, she had nowhere else to go and she was starving.

Morosely, she stabbed her arms into the fluffy bathrobe from the peg in the bathroom and placed the sign hanging from the pocket on the vanity, which read, *Help yourself to this complimentary robe. We will gladly charge your room for it.*

Everything cost something. That was the lesson here. So she'd wear it for now, and put it back neatly the way she found it. At least wearing the robe, she felt more like she belonged in this luxurious suite.

She eased the door open and tiptoed out into the main living area. The year of living quietly with Daddy's drunken rages had honed her ability to creep through any room with the finesse of a jewel thief.

"Can't sleep?"

Kris's voice cut through the black, and VJ yelped. An exhale of breath, low and even, came from the direction of one of the trim couches, indiscernible in the dark.

"Hungry," she said, and cleared her throat. "I was hoping the refrigerator had something in it."

"It does. Champagne." His voice snaked around her, burrowing under the robe to kiss her bare skin. "What are you hungry for? I'll order room service."

Before she told him exactly what she hungered for, she asked, "Why are you awake? I was expecting you to be in your room." *Or I never would have left mine.*

"Blocking scenes in my head. I have a whacked out creative process, which works best in pitch-black with no distractions. Bed is for sleeping."

Full dark did something sinful to his accent. It was more pronounced and breaking at odd intervals. Fatigue, no doubt, and not due to the same heavy awareness messing with *her* voice.

"Sorry I intruded, then." She started to back away and tripped, almost swan-diving into the unfamiliar low-pile carpet. Thankfully, the lack of light hid her graceless recovery.

"You didn't. Stay. This is your room, too. I don't want you to feel like a guest who can't be hungry."

His disembodied voice was disturbing as it spiraled around inside her, heating places it couldn't be allowed to affect. He needed to be with Kyla, and she needed more than one night. Melancholy lodged behind her breastbone. "Can you at least turn on a light? I'm not part cat."

Some shuffling and muted light spilled into the room from the half circle of windows as he drew back the drapes. He'd changed into a pair of soft pants which clung to every line of his hips and thighs. And he was shirtless.

Her tummy tumbled to Mexico. The glow of skyscrapers rippled along his shoulders and his lean torso as he tucked the heavy curtains aside. His arms were as sculpted as his face, bulging slightly with muscle, tendons wrapping to his wrist in a trail she'd follow any day.

"Um, maybe dark was better," she blurted and smacked her forehead. *Shut up.*

"I disagree. I like that tousled look on you."

He disappeared into his room and returned covered up by a shirt and she stifled a sigh. Well, the image of his bare back was emblazoned across her retinas like lightning forking through the sky, shirt or no shirt. In what world did someone so charismatic and finely built end up behind the camera?

"I'll order us something. I haven't eaten, either," he said as he settled back onto the couch as if nothing had happened. Nothing *had* happened, but she was still frozen four feet from her door.

It was just dinner. She'd eaten two other meals with Kris. But neither of those meals had taken place behind closed doors while she wore nothing other than a big towel.

"Sit down." He nodded to the empty cushion a quarter inch from his thigh and picked up the phone from the end table. "You're not bothering me. Really."

You're bothering me.

Cautiously, she edged onto the couch—the other couch—and tugged the robe up around her neck as a flimsy barrier.

The tranquil sage and deep purples artfully strewn about the suite invited her to relax, to enjoy the rare reprieve from taking care of Daddy and her brothers, but the oasis had no effect on her goose bumps. Or the grasshoppers in her stomach. This was entirely too intimate, and she had no business being here with an almost-engaged man.

Even if he wasn't going to marry Kyla. Especially if he wasn't.

Nothing good ever happened after midnight. This was the time of night when Cinderella was still hobbling home, minus a shoe and toting a fourteen-pound pumpkin. Good Baptists were in bed. Asleep.

They sat in edgy silence for an eternity.

"I've been wondering," he said, startling her out of a fantasy where she'd stripped him of all his clothes and straddled him, still wearing the robe, but loosening the sash enough for it to slip off one shoulder.

"Hmm?"

"What's stage six?"

Her heart stumbled over a beat. "I'll tell you tomorrow."

"What's wrong with now?"

Where should she start counting all the reasons why not now? "It's late, and you're working."

"I'm done. Why are you sitting way over there?"

"I like this couch. It's comfortable. That one is too small for two people. With your long legs and all." God, she was babbling.

"My legs aren't on the couch."

He sounded amused, and why wouldn't he be? She was laughably inexperienced at sitting around in the half-light of a bustling urban city with a sophisticated man almost engaged to someone else.

"What's stage six?" he asked again, and merciful heaven, a knock at the door signaled the arrival of dinner. She sprang for the door before he could move.

A white-coated waiter stood in the hall with a rolling cart, staring at her expectantly. Kris materialized behind her, pressing the length of his taut frame against hers, leaning into it. Her breath rattled in her throat as the shock of awareness, the heat of his body, thrummed through her.

Then Kris gently guided her from the doorway to allow the waiter to roll the cart inside. Her breath rushed out in a sigh. She'd been in the way. That's all. This roller coaster of hope and dashed hope was getting ridiculous.

Ridiculous because she shouldn't have any hopes except to get her life settled and move on.

Kris tipped the waiter and moved the dishes from the dining area to the low coffee table shared by the couches. "Is this okay? I hate eating formally. Reminds me too much of when I lived with my parents."

"Sure." She wasn't going to be able to swallow anything anyway. Then he lifted the metal cover from one of the plates. Fried chicken. She almost laughed, until the meaty smell of it weakened her knees. Okay, so she'd eat a little something.

Five pieces later, she couldn't shove anything else in her mouth with a pitchfork.

Kris reclined on the floor opposite her, licking his fingers, and she avoided another stray glance at his tongue. Too late. Heat gathered in her core as she recalled the way he'd devoured her at the top of the Ferris wheel. He'd done something wicked with his mouth, drawing her tongue into it and sucking, but she'd felt it between her legs simultaneously.

"Is it tomorrow yet?" he asked, and she glanced at him.

He was watching her, his eyelids low and sexy as if well sated after a good, hard roll in silk sheets. Why did he have to be so hot?

"It'll be dawn soon. I guess that makes it tomorrow."

"Then what's stage six?"

"What's the fascination with stage six?"

What was her fascination with his mouth? She couldn't stop staring at it. She wanted to keep him talking but this was the wrong subject.

"The best way to get me interested in something is to withhold it. Curiosity isn't only hazardous to felines."

Bingo. The secret to romancing Kris was to withhold. And keep withholding until he was exploding with need. She sighed. Useless information now. "Of course. You don't really care what stage six is. You just care that I know something you don't."

He grinned and leaned back against the couch, legs spread underneath the coffee table. "Exactly."

Lights from the window threw his body into relief. Hair fell into his face against the fine planes of his cheekbones, and she sat on her hands before she did something really ill-advised. Only a dimwit licked a battery twice. "Well, you know lots of things I don't. How is that fair?"

"Trade you, then. Tell me about stage six, and I'll tell you something you don't know."

Suspicious, she planted her elbows on the low table and leaned forward. "No deal. It's late, and I'm tired."

She wasn't. She'd never been more awake—aware—in her life. There was a coffee table between them but it provided no barricade against the spark of his presence.

Gracefully, he edged across the carpet and tipped her head up with the finger that, seconds ago, had been in his mouth. His heat branded her chin and she wasn't so sure she had it in her to withhold anything from him.

He peered into her eyes. "What's going on in there? Are you afraid of something?"

"Kris. Please don't touch me."

"You are afraid. Of me." His shoulders slumped as he dropped his hand to the floor. "I don't want you to be afraid. Would you prefer a separate room?"

"No!" Had she shouted? "I mean, I'm not scared of you. This whole middle-of-the-night scenario just isn't proper. You're about to be engaged, and we've already…done things. Things we shouldn't have. I know I gave you the wrong impression, but I'm not some wild woman out for a good time with the first man I find."

"I don't think that." He reclined into a different position. Closer. He extended his long legs behind her and propped up his head on his palm as if they were having a slumber party instead of a Come To Jesus about this electric attraction boiling the atmosphere.

She rolled her eyes. "Why wouldn't you? I attacked you. On the Ferris wheel."

"Well, I was warned you'd take advantage of me at the first

opportunity." He was fighting a smile. "It's my own fault I allowed myself to fall into your clutches. Would you feel better if I told you I knew what you were up to at the carnival?"

No, she would have preferred to continue deluding herself about how clever she was. But obviously that ship had sailed.

"Kris." She couldn't keep up this back-and-forth dance. "You have to do the engagement, and I can't be your dirty secret, hiding in the extra room and pretending to be your assistant or whatever. There can't be anything between us. That's why we can't talk about stage six."

His entire body stiffened, and she was ashamed to have noticed.

"I never intended to make you feel like a dirty secret when I offered the extra room. I'm sorry," he said. Sincerity deepened the hollows along his cheekbones. "We could have avoided all this if you'd taken my trade."

"What trade? Oh, where I tell you about stage six and you tell me something?" She exhaled. Well, she'd laid it all out there, and he'd apologized instead of laughing. What's the worst that could happen now? "Fine. Dazzle me."

Eyes dark and unfathomable, he stared at her. Slowly, he reached out to take her hand. He laced their fingers together and with a lift of his chin, he said, "You first. Stop being so cagey about stage six. Tell me what it is."

His thumb traced her knuckles in a crazy, sensual pattern, and her brain shut down. At least that was her excuse for being so stupid as to continue this dangerous game of romance instruction. Being struck brainless had to be the reason she opened her mouth and whispered, "Consummation."

His hand tightened and an elemental shock blistered up her arm as his expression heated. "I like stage six."

She was trapped in his gaze, trapped by his touch. He lifted her hand to his mouth and watched her with clear intent as his lips molded around the tips of her fingers in a kiss.

"That wasn't a suggestion. It's only a word. We're just talking." She yanked her hand from his and desperation set in. He had to stop crawling inside her with that hooded expression, as if he'd been stranded on a desert island and she was water. "I'm not trying to convince you of anything anymore. You can get engaged to Kyla with a clear conscience. I give you my blessing. Now I told you about stage six. It's your turn."

He sat up and his presence spread, creeping into all the molecules around her until she was overwhelmed. "The engagement," he said and waited until she met his eyes, quite against her will, before continuing. "Isn't happening. I'm calling it off."

The room snapped out of focus. "What?"

"It's nothing more than a publicity stunt. A stupid one, at that. I won't go through with it."

Okay, she'd kind of already pieced together the publicity thing. But suddenly *bloodless* seemed too tame to describe such a cold business proposition, especially when applied to the institution of marriage.

"Wait." Her head spun. "Is this because of all the things I said about romance and being in love? Am I *that* convincing?"

"You're very convincing. But I never wanted to do it in the first place even though I saw the potential benefit." He shrugged. "I decided it wasn't worth it after all."

"Just now you decided?" His nod answered that question. "But your career. Kris, you can't give up your movie."

"I'm not. There has to be another way. And I'll find it." He wouldn't let her look away. "Please keep this between us. I can't stop you from telling the media. But I'm asking you not to."

"I'm not going to say anything." What would she say when none of this revelation made a lick of sense? "Why are you telling me this?"

Please let him say he wanted to remove all the obstacles, in true heroic fashion, before sweeping her into his arms, professing his feelings and making love to her all night.

This was it, where fantasy became reality. Her pulse leaped like a gazelle. She was so underdressed.

"Because. I don't want you to be upset about kissing me or about being here with me in a hotel room. The whole day was a blast. The most fun I've had in a long time. Let's keep going."

Fun.

The fried chicken churned greasily through her stomach. He was calling off the engagement because he didn't want to do it. Not because she'd unlocked him and he couldn't live without a fulfilling relationship a second longer.

"So," he continued, oblivious to the crushing anvil pressing on her chest. "Door's wide-open while I'm in Dallas. You've still got me in your clutches. Feel free to take advantage of me anytime."

How romantic. Not only had nothing she'd said penetrated, he expected her to make the first move while he kept his heart nice and safe behind the wall marked No Trespassing. He was testing the waters to see if she might be up for a little no-strings-attached fling while he was in town.

"I have to get some sleep," she whispered. "Two sleepless nights in a row might kill me." If the poisoned arrows in her heart didn't do the job first.

"Sure," he said as she stumbled to her feet and fled for the bedroom.

With a quiet click, she closed the door. Spine against oak, she slid to the floor in a heap of terry-cloth robe and bit her lip, but the pain didn't eclipse the hurt stinging through her heart.

Really, what had she expected?

Wait a minute.

She sat bolt upright. Kris might pretend to be a casual sex kind of guy, but if he really thought she was an easy target for a fling, tonight had been the perfect opportunity for seduction, with close quarters and various states of undress. Why hadn't he gone ahead?

She crawled to the bed and climbed into it. He hadn't because he'd wanted to put the power in her hands.

The power to what? Agree to a blistering liaison and then kiss him goodbye in a few days? What exactly *did* he want?

Chewing on her lip, she stared at the shut door, but her X-ray vision hadn't improved. Yet she knew what was on the other side. Furniture. Carpet. Kris. Just like she knew what lay beyond the wall protecting Kris's heart.

He lied to himself about not believing in love. Insisted he'd enter into a loveless business-arrangement engagement when he obviously couldn't. Expended an enormous amount of energy suppressing his passionate nature. He piled all of it on top of that wall, keeping everyone out and himself in.

His greatest emotional need was to embrace the passion he kept buried, and he wanted—needed—her to shove him past that point of no return. It was the only way he'd crack, and his relationship with Kyla had been in the way. So he'd removed it from the equation. Expecting her to do the math.

But what if Greek math wasn't the same as West Texas math, and she'd misread the situation? She thumped the pillow with a fist. She couldn't be wrong. No way. His engine might be wired a little differently than most men, but she'd bet everything she had exactly the right key to start it.

It was a dare.

Subtly, he was asking if she was woman enough to rise to the challenge of winning his heart.

The answer was yes. Yes, she was.

Eight

After an excellent night of sleep, Kris flipped on the water in the shower and experienced a moment of pure shock when he realized the buoyancy to his step was happiness.

VJ was so unlike other women. Challenging. Provoking. Exciting. He loved being around her. He hadn't consciously planned to ditch the engagement, but she'd been so broken up about kissing him, the words had fallen out of his mouth. And the weight lifted instantly.

He hated the idea of manipulating the public with a fictitious engagement between the star and the director of a movie. How had it taken this long to realize it? There had to be a different publicity angle because he wasn't doing the fake engagement. Now or ever. A desert mirage in an orange pickup truck had knocked some sense into his head.

What was wrong with selling tickets by promoting *Visions of Black* as a good film? He'd gladly work eighteen hours a day to generate that kind of publicity. Talk shows, viral campaigns via the internet, free early screenings. He'd find something Abrams and Kyla could agree to, even if he had to walk Ventura Boulevard with a bullhorn.

Kyla was going to be royally pissed but he'd deal with it. *Visions* would be good for her career, and she'd see that. He'd help her see that.

With all the complications out of the way, he could focus on VJ. He wanted to pick up where that Ferris-wheel kiss had ended. Right now.

Given her serious romantic fantasies, five bucks said *temporary* wasn't in her vocabulary. *Permanent* wasn't in his. Couldn't be in his. Which meant he had to back off. Way off. He'd laid out his availability for whatever she could cook up. Now it was up to her to decide if she'd jump into a short-term affair. She had to make the move. Period.

He got out of the shower, ran a brush through his hair and dressed quickly, eager to see VJ and not about to apologize for it. When he emerged from his room, she was sitting at the table, staring out the window at the downtown vista. Rush-hour haze still smudged the tops of the skyscrapers, though it was nearing noon.

"Good morning," he said.

Her hair was damp, as if she'd recently emerged from the shower, as well. Where she'd been naked and wet. Not a good image to fixate on before coffee and after deciding to back off.

"Hey." She didn't even glance at him.

Okay. Calling off the engagement should have eliminated tension, not added it.

He tried again. "What's on your agenda for the day?"

"Job hunting. I guess." Her posture put steel to shame, and her hands were clenched into a tight ball in her lap.

The day had started off with such promise—at least on his part. Where had all the easy intimacy between them gone? Out the window, apparently, now that he'd drawn the short-term-only line.

He'd known it would likely go this way, but, selfishly, he

wanted the spark without having to promise her more. As brightly as the attraction burned between them, he'd have a hard enough time keeping himself under control in the short-term.

"Didn't you mention in the car earlier that tomorrow is your birthday?" At her hesitant nod, he pulled out his phone and checked his schedule. "That calls for a celebration. Let me take you to dinner tonight."

"Thanks. Maybe some other time."

Some other time. He'd expected a resounding *no*. He hadn't expected it to suck so much. "Come on. It'll be fun."

"Kris." She shut her eyes for a beat. "I don't have anything to wear."

Of course she didn't. Instantly, he scrapped all his plans for the day, including the two hours he'd blocked to check out casting videos his assistant had sent. Some sacrifices were worth it. VJ deserved more than just dinner. She deserved a fairy tale, and he was going to give her one, whether she agreed to short-term or not. "I'll take you shopping. Consider it part of your birthday present."

Finally, she swiveled. "Don't guys hate shopping?"

He shrugged. "Yeah. I hate traffic, too, but it's unavoidable if I want to get somewhere."

"So shopping is a means to an end?"

Her tone prickled the back of his neck. "An unfortunate analogy. I'm fully prepared for you to shut your door at the end of the night." There was nothing wrong, however, with hoping they'd be on the same side of the door. "I want to do something nice for you. Is that really so awful?"

"No. It's not." Suddenly, she smiled, and the light returned to her face, thumping him right between the eyes. That alone was worth getting behind on his long task list.

"Then let's go. We can get lunch on the way."

He took her to a boutique close to the hotel and turned VJ over to a sales clerk. They disappeared into another section of the store and returned quickly, just as he'd settled into a plush chair to wait. The sales clerk had several garments draped over her arm so either VJ made up her mind really fast—and if so, he'd nominate her for woman of the year—or the clerk had selected them.

Eventually, VJ emerged from behind the divided panel, flustered and adorable, with nothing in her hands. "Are you sure about this?"

"Very sure. Pick out a dress. Pick two." Kris scouted around for the clerk. "Miss? She needs shoes and everything else a woman requires for a night out. *Everything.* Also, can you write down the name of a good spa?"

A blush spread over VJ's cheeks. "For what?"

"So you can spend the day being spoiled. Don't even think about saying no." He guided her in the direction of the clerk and crossed his arms so he couldn't yank her to him and kiss her senseless.

His hands tightened into fists. Backing off was harder than he'd anticipated.

Playing chauffeur for the rest of the afternoon gave him plenty of downtime to make reservations and get directions. The spa took a couple of hours, so he squeezed in the casting videos, not at all annoyed to view them on the small screen of his phone instead of his laptop.

"Dinner's at eight," he told VJ when she slid into the Ferrari after the spa session. "Will that work?"

"Sure." She put a hand over his on the gear shift. "Thanks. I'm having a great day. Four people worked on me at the same time, like I was royalty. The experience was truly wonderful."

They'd put some kind of lotion on her hands, softening her skin.

"Yeah? I'm glad." That creamy expanse of throat above the neckline of her T-shirt caught his attention. Now he was wondering if her skin was that same kind of soft all over and what it smelled like.

"I know you don't expect anything in return. But I got you a little something anyway." She smiled mischievously.

"What is it?"

"It's a surprise, for later. Your favorite color is red, right?" The pad of her finger slid up a tendon in his hand, following the corded line up his arm. His pulse tripped.

"How did you know?"

"I guessed. Wasn't hard. Red's the color of passion. Take me back to the hotel now?"

Take me echoed in his head, and the close atmosphere in the car stirred along his skin. Her eyes were luminous, and her fingers still played with his arm, feeling the crease at the bend of his elbow, swirling along his muscles. Then she lightly skimmed his shoulder and slid fingers into his hair, setting his nerve endings on fire.

He sucked in a hot breath and eased closer, into her space. "If you want to kiss me again, all you have to do is say so."

The blue around her pupils swam with flecks of yellow and glinted when she licked her lips in a slow glide. "Same goes."

Her thumb cruised along his jaw, then rested on his bottom lip with feather-light contact and the tip of her nail grazed it. The impact tightened the base of his spine and spread with tendrils of warmth.

"You have an amazing mouth, Kristian." Her own mouth was slack, forming that *O* he longed to fill.

With an encouraging nibble of his lips, her thumb slid deep in his mouth. As he sucked on it, her eyelids fluttered closed and that awesome moan vibrated in her throat. His groin flooded, tight and hot.

That was it.

He plucked her thumb away and caught her mouth in a kiss. Her hands clutched his shoulders, pulling him closer. Her tongue met his in a hot rush and they twined. He needed her, needed more, and reached for it.

His elbow hit the steering wheel. They were in the car. Kyla's Ferrari, for God's sake.

This was the exact opposite of backing off.

He started to break away and couldn't. One more second against her mouth was all he needed. He slanted his lips at the opposite angle, tilted her head back and relentlessly drank from her.

More.

No. Not more.

He jerked away. He had more control than this. He had to find it. Problem was, he'd never needed to find it. It had never failed before.

"Italian for dinner?" he rasped, his vocal cords dry with need. He shifted into first and tried, unsuccessfully, to ignore the ache in his gut.

"Sure," she said with a small smile.

When they got back to the hotel, she sauntered to her room, hands full of bags, leaving him at loose ends. Aimlessly, he wandered to the couch and flipped on the TV, trying to will away the semi hard-on he'd had since the car.

Time stood still as he relived the Ferris-wheel kiss. Then the car kiss. And back again, until his almost hard-on turned into a raging one.

The images, the ache. VJ. The swirl became a continual persistence of vision he couldn't control, couldn't dissolve from his mind's eye. He had an incredible amount of work to do and yet, here he sat like a horny seventeen-year-old.

"Kris," VJ called from the bedroom. "Can you help me with something?"

Of course. Because what better way to settle his hormones than to be in VJ's bedroom? Where there was a bed. With sheets smelling of coconut.

"Down, boy," he muttered.

VJ was going to have a romantic evening if it killed him. Her future did not include telling some other guy about how

Kris Demetrious didn't speak the same language as romance. His Greek was more than passable if he did say so himself.

He stalked into her room. She stood in the middle of it wearing that virginal white robe, loosely belted, falling off one shoulder.

So it *was* going to kill him.

One breast swelled above the neckline, practically inviting him to delve into the V created by the folds of fabric. Miles of legs extended beyond the hem and led to bare feet. Red toenails dug into the carpet, all but begging to be licked. Begging him to keep going, licking up her smooth legs, straight to what was under that sexy robe.

"What do you need me for?" he asked. Since she was dressed, clearly it wasn't the same thing he needed her for.

She rattled her arms and the robe's sash slipped, exposing a pale swatch of skin. Was she naked under there? He couldn't tear his eyes off that tantalizing glimpse of VJ's flesh.

"Which one should I wear tonight?" she said. "I don't know where we're going."

Out of the corner of his eye, he noticed she had a dress in each hand.

"That one." He pointed without looking away from the gap under the robe's sash.

"I like that one, too." She threw both dresses on the bed and grasped the knot holding the slim belt's ends together.

His legs went numb as she worked to untie it. *Untie. It.* So he could greedily drink in the sight of her uncovered body. Naked before him, ripe and gorgeous.

Anticipation burned through his midsection. Could she labor over that tangle of sash any more leisurely?

Finally, it was loose. With agonizing slowness, she opened the robe. A flash of nipple seared his vision. Immediately, she drew the robe closed, tightening it around her waist, then tying the sash into a firm knot with quick-fingered precision. She turned away. "Thanks for your help. I'll be ready by eight."

He'd been dismissed. Soundly. And it was at least an hour until eight.

Time for a really, really cold shower. Which did not cool his blood. Or slow his pulse. Or reduce the burn of his erection. As he stood under the icy spray, he reshot that scene with an entirely different story line, where he laid her back against the carpet and untied that knot with his teeth. Then he'd spread her legs wide to drink from that well he'd been denied for far too long. He'd slide into her easily because she was so hot and slick for him, and she'd be quaking with that sexy little moan.

Yeah, like that. Again and again, until they exploded. Back-handing hair out of his eyes, he sagged against the frigid glass tiles and suffered.

Why didn't he blast into her room and take her, right there on the floor? Up against the wall. Bent over the dresser. All of the above. A consummation to end all consummations.

Moron. Not only would his creativity in the bedroom scare her blind, he was backing off. She'd get her a special evening, the kind she could remember reverently forever. There were no fairy tales where the prince subjected the princess to a rutting sexual offensive. No real women liked that, either.

It had just never been as difficult to remain detached as it was with VJ.

This was why he stayed behind the camera. Once uncorked, his passions ran over without restraint. He had to find a way to flip that switch back into the off position. He was not his father, who was so ruled by his passions that he allowed them to turn ugly.

Intelligent, funny, in-your-face Victoria Jane Lewis, who'd never left Texas because she'd unselfishly committed to caring for her sick mother, deserved better.

The stages of romance meant something to her. VJ's greatest emotional need was to star in her own fairy tale. So he'd keep his hands off of her until he could take her to dinner and treat her like a princess. Period.

* * *

After stressing over her makeup until it adequately covered the not-quite-faded bruise, VJ slithered into the black dress and blocked out the rushing sound of Mama turning over in her grave. Again.

The dress was designed for sin. Backless and form fitting, it dipped into a low heart shape over her cleavage. Under it, see-through crimson lace cradled her breasts and smooshed them skyward. The clerk at the boutique had spent Kris's money easy-peasy.

How could she have predicted it would put her on edge? Surely Kris had a little less respect for her because she couldn't have purchased any of this on her own. She couldn't ask him to come back later, when she was stable. Then she wouldn't have needed rescue. They probably wouldn't have ever met.

Fate had intervened, pushing them together. She and Kris were kindred souls. Romantics in a world designed to bleed it out of them. Instead of embracing it, he hid his true passionate nature from everyone, apparently clueless that it leaked out all over his films. His choice of music. His heroic defense against her brothers. The way he kissed with his whole body.

If she could convince him to accept that passion, all the obstacles to his heart would be gone. He had to be the one to make the move, to be so overcome, he gave in.

Unfortunately, Kris wasn't any closer to cracking than he'd been all along. For a moment, in the car, she'd thought she'd had him, but no. Then after the nerve-racking robe retying debacle—maybe she wasn't cut out for this.

"Amateur," she whispered to her reflection. He needed a huge push. Bigger than the Ferris wheel, but more effective, with longer lasting results.

Her tummy fluttered. She wanted to be with him something fierce, to see straight into his soul through those limitless eyes because she was the only one he let in. She wanted to fall the rest of the way in love, and if she did her job, he'd be right behind her. When that happened, everything would merge. The future, last names, hearts. That was the real dream come true.

One push coming up.

The black stilettos took fifteen minutes of practice before she could walk in them without stumbling. She wobbled out of her bedroom. Kris sat at the table, tapping at his laptop, and glanced up when she called his name.

His expression darkened as his molten brown eyes did a once-over all the way to her toes, devouring her with his heated gaze. Her thighs pressed together involuntarily against the throb under her brand-new thong.

Without speaking, he shoved the chair back with his thighs and crossed the room. Grasping her hand, he spun her in a slow pirouette. Heat crept up her spine as he took in the backless dress.

"That," he said, "was worth waiting for. I'm almost speechless. You're stunning."

"Thanks." She ducked her head, suddenly embarrassed at the raw desire on his face. Since that had been the whole point of the dress, her reaction made no sense, but he'd been around lots of beautiful women. Surely she paled in comparison.

"Do you have your lipstick in your bag?" he asked.

He drew her closer so he could slide a hand around her neck, resting his fingers lightly on her flesh. She shuddered. "Am I supposed to?"

"Yeah. You're going to need it."

He lowered his head and kissed her. Her eyes shut as he flooded her with the beauty of his skill. When Kristian Demetrious kissed her, it killed her equilibrium.

His clever hands explored her bare back, warming it, sensitizing it. He pressed her against his frame, tight. The tiny pulls of his lips were slow, sensual, with simmering potential. But the kiss lacked abandon, winding down instead of ramping up.

Not so fast.

She shimmied her hips against his with an upward tilt, finding that perfect hard niche where they fit together, and rubbed against his solid chest as she angled her head to let him take her deeper.

Instead, he broke away, taking an unsteady step back and a ragged breath at the same time. "Remind me later to buy you several more pairs of those shoes. I really, really like you at that height."

With her stomach twisting like a tornado, she motioned him over. "Come back. See what I got you."

Warily, he edged closer. With one finger, she hooked the neckline of the dress and pulled it down, revealing the tiny, red butterfly tattoo a centimeter from her nipple.

His eyes went black as he zeroed in on her exposed breast, and he strangled on whatever he was trying to say. Now he was completely speechless.

She was going to hell. With bells on.

After smoothing the dress back into place, she said, "I'm starving. Ready? Where are we going?"

"I don't remember. Give me a minute," he said shortly and stared at the ceiling, running a trembling hand through his hair. "Get your lipstick."

His accent was frayed, and it tingled her spine. She wanted to hear him say something really provocative with that voice, preferably while touching her.

She gathered her things and brushed the bulge in his pants as she walked past him through the door. He sucked in a shuddery breath but didn't say anything. The butterfly had clearly produced results, but not the one she'd envisioned.

She needed to up her game even more. But how?

Casa di Luigi was the height of fine dining, with white-on-black tablecloths, more silverware at each place than she set for a family of four and endless numbers of servers who waited on them. Kris ordered red wine, and when it came, he watched her over the wineglass rim with a shadowy, hooded expression as he drank.

Muted clinks and murmurs of conversation floated around them, but they weren't talking. Instead, a nonverbal swirl of innuendo crackled between them.

He set his glass on the table without breaking eye contact and picked up her hand. "Are you having a good time?"

"The best. This is a great restaurant."

"Tell me more about your book," he said out of nowhere. "What was it called?"

"Which one? *Embrace the Rogue?*"

"The one with Lord Raven. What's it about?"

"Lord Ravenwood." She narrowed her eyes. "Why do you want to know what it's about?"

"I want to talk about something that interests you."

She shrugged. "It's about a duke who rescues a lady from a runaway carriage and it's love at first sight. Except he's... what?"

"That's what it's about?"

"What did you think it was? A more explicit, unillustrated version of the *Kama Sutra?*"

Kris choked on a sip of wine and took his time recovering. "What do you know about the *Kama Sutra?*"

"It's a book, isn't it?" She stared at him with a ghost of a smile. He'd started tracing her knuckles restlessly, but his eyes were fixed on her face. "Why, have you read it?"

"I have."

The expectation sizzling through the air heightened. He brought her hand to his lips and lightly grazed the tips of her fingers. The shock traveled up her arm like a deluge swelling over the banks of the Rio Grande.

Then he said, "I can't figure you out."

"At last, my dastardly plan to be a woman of mystery has been fulfilled." She could hardly keep her attention on the conversation as he nibbled her index finger. "Why does it seem like my fingers are always in your mouth?"

"Because I like the taste of you, and we're in public. This is the best I can do."

She closed her eyes against the rush of need spiraling through her abdomen. If he kept that up, she wouldn't be doing a whole lot of withholding much longer.

Time to go on the offensive. He needed to make a move and do it soon or she would be forced to end this evening in a chaste kiss good-night at nine o'clock.

"So, about the *Kama Sutra,*" she said and leaned forward. The edge of the table shoved her bra down a centimeter. What little it had covered originally had already been pornographic. "Which one is your favorite?"

"Position?" His hand trembled and he pointedly kept his eyes on her face.

She gave him a look. "Yes, Sherlock. Position."

A strangled sound launched from his throat. "Seriously? It's not enough that I can't erase the vivid picture in my head of what's underneath that dress?"

"You started it with the tasting me in public," she whispered in deference to the elderly couple at the next table.

Kris waved the beleaguered waiter away and tightened his grip on her hand. "Fine. You go first. What's yours?"

"I don't know. I haven't tried them all yet." She lifted a brow. "I'm in the market for a guinea pig actually."

His breath hissed out and he let go of her hand. "This is not working."

Then he made a show of examining his flatware. She folded her hands into her lap. Obviously she shouldn't assume she could handle Kristian Demetrious.

"VJ," he said, eyes still on the tines of the fork flipping between his first two fingers. "Help me out. This is your birthday present. A nice dinner. Dancing later. I'm following the stages. And I'm asking you nicely to stop talking about sex so we can have the romantic evening I've planned. Would you like to order dinner now?"

Following the stages? Her heart squeezed. So that's why he'd asked about *Embrace the Rogue*. "No. I really don't want dinner."

"What would you like to do, then? I'm taking you dancing at a place that plays country music. We can go there now if you want and eat later."

Warmth spread through her chest. He remembered what kind of music she liked and was willing to endure it for a few hours. For her. Kris had been trying to show her she'd infiltrated his disbelief in romance. It was a huge move, and she'd almost missed it because it hadn't taken the form she'd expected.

"I'd be happy to help you out," she said decisively. "Take me back to the hotel right now, or I'm never going to speak to you again."

His intense gaze lasered in on hers, evaluating. "Then it's okay to skip all the stages and dive right into bed?"

She swallowed a laugh. Did he really not realize? Or was romance so much a part of his nature, he'd done it unwittingly? "You didn't skip any stages. You hit them all. I'm yours."

More evaluating. "I'll take you back to the hotel if that's what you want. But, VJ, be sure. I'm still leaving to go back to L.A. in a few days."

Not if I have anything to say about it.

She crossed her fingers under the table. If he wanted to keep pretending this was some casual encounter, she could, too. Whatever worked to shove him closer to embracing all the beautiful things he deserved. All the things they could have together.

"I'm clear. We're just having fun, right?"

His mouth twitched. "Where do I volunteer to be a guinea pig?"

His wicked grin kick-started her lungs again.

He met her eyes and a shock of lust uncurled deep in her core as he skewered her with probing intensity. Kris always had a slight sensual edge but it was fundamental to the way he moved and spoke. A fluke of his DNA. This was different. Lashing desire radiated from him, and she couldn't look away.

"I can't wait to find out what your butterfly tastes like," he said. "Last chance to back out."

She went hot and cold simultaneously, and squirmed against the heat licking through her. "Give the waiter your credit card."

"I have cash." He yanked his wallet out of his pocket and tossed a hundred on the table. "How fast can you walk in those heels?"

"Bet you can't keep up," she said and sprang to her feet at the same instant he did.

Nine

The atmosphere during the drive to the hotel was thick with impatience. Kris skidded into a parking place and materialized at her door to help her out, then pulled her through the lobby to the elevator. He stabbed the button, and the doors slid open.

It was empty. As the doors closed, Kris whirled her against the back of the elevator and crushed his mouth to hers. An edge of violent desperation flavored his kiss, thrilling her. His hands were everywhere as he consumed her. He tongued his way down the curve of her neck, yanked her dress down and licked a nipple into his mouth.

Her head lolled back and hit the wall, but she barely noticed as he sucked her nipple hard with the same pulling sensation he always used with her tongue. Heat raged through her, between her legs and down her thighs, and she moaned.

His fingers snaked up the back of her leg, then burned across her bare bottom. He dipped under the straps holding her thong in place.

One finger eased along her crease, parting and thrusting

against the wetness there. Consciousness nearly dissolved with the heightened sensation. His hands were magic, driving deep, filling her, fulfilling her. She thrust against the pressure, and the spiral inside tightened as his mouth switched to her other breast, treating it to the same perfect suction as the other. Then he nibbled on her nipple.

She bucked against his hand.

"Kris... Kris. Stop," she choked out with gasping little breaths, nearly weeping as his mouth left her flesh.

"Why in God's name should I do that?" he snapped.

She yanked on his shoulders until he straightened. "Because we're at our floor. Let's go inside."

His eyelids slammed shut. "Sorry," he mumbled. "I got carried away."

The elevator doors slid open. His obvious chagrin was endearing, but she couldn't for the life of her figure out why getting carried away was bad.

Without a word, he tucked her breasts away and led her out of the elevator. Smoothly, he slid the card key into the reader, pushed the door open and swept her up in his arms to carry her over the threshold and into his bedroom.

Elephants stampeded through her stomach. Rose petals were strewn all over the bed in a wholly romantic gesture. Her heart was lost. Probably had been since the first time he smiled at her on Little Crooked Creek Road.

Oh, God, what if she hadn't recognized the stages? She'd never have known about the rose petals.

He set her down carefully, and without warning, hooked the shoulder straps of her dress and peeled it off, trapping her arms with the fabric.

"That is more like it," he said with appreciation.

He looked his fill, studying her breasts—clearly visible through the transparent bra—with marked intensity, eyes hot and his gaze never wavering, until her cheeks were on fire. The butterfly had him mesmerized.

"I'm not a Monet," she squawked, which was not the sexy voice she'd been going for.

"You are. You're exquisite. And you have on too many clothes." The dress was around her ankles instantly. "Red's not actually my favorite color, by the way."

"It's not?" Dang it. She *knew* she shouldn't have gone with the permanent tattoo. "What is?"

He placed one finger on the edge of the thong and pushed it down. Way down, and then grazed her nub with a knuckle. "That is. I want to see it."

Wet heat pooled around his finger as he rubbed it back and forth. A long wave of desire crested and broke at his touch. He worked the finger inside her folds and then withdrew, pulling a hiss from her. She grabbed at his shoulders when her knees buckled.

"You can see it all you want," she said breathlessly. "But you have to do something for me."

"What's that?"

"Talk to me with that incredible voice." He went deep, and her inner walls clenched tight, and she moaned. "Kristian."

His eyes darkened. "I cannot tell you what it does to me when you say that."

"Try."

He smiled and pulled her close. He nuzzled her ear and whispered a long string of Greek as he unhooked her bra, which he threw over his shoulder. Still murmuring, he backed her up until her thighs hit the bed. He sat her down. Somehow her thong was gone, too.

He knelt between her legs and watched her as he put his mouth where his finger had been. He did that sucking thing, like with her tongue, but against her nub and mouthed some more Greek intermittently, lips brushing her as he enunciated.

Part of her tried to pull away from the intimacy. She'd never be able to look him in the eye again, but oh, it was amazing, and she started to splinter, scooting her hips forward, involuntarily seeking his miraculous mouth.

Her head thrashed back and forth as he sucked and licked and murmured foreign words and drove her off the edge. Her spine curved as she erupted, and heat rippled from the epicenter of her climax.

He kissed her thigh, and she fell back onto the comforter, so sated her bones were like melted chocolate. He crawled up to lie next to her, and she was ashamed to note he still wore all his clothes.

"Talk to you like that?" His hands wandered into her hair, tangling it through his fingers as he stroked her jawline tenderly with a thumb.

How in the world had she gotten so incredibly lucky as to be lying naked on a bed with Kristian Demetrious?

"Exactly like that." Her breath came in spurts. "And may I say you are extremely talented at…um, talking. But there's this other thing I need you to do, too."

In a daring move, she rolled and crawled on top of him, straddling him in that niche where they fit together, hip to hip. The man was hard all over, and she was dying to feel every golden millimeter.

His breath caught. "How talented do you think I am?"

"Let's put it to the test." She crushed a rose petal between her fingers and trailed it over his chiseled lips. "Next time I come, I want you inside me."

Eyes closed, he wound up great bunches of comforter in his tight fists. "You're making this very hard."

She wiggled against his still-covered erection. "Isn't that the idea?"

"Stop." He stilled her hips with a firm hand on each one. "You're driving me insane. I'm trying to do this right, and you're not playing your part."

"Oh? Maybe you should give me a script, Mr. Director. What should I be doing instead?"

"This is supposed to be *your* romantic fantasy evening, not mine." His voice rumbled against her pleasantly. "So far, we haven't eaten dinner, we didn't go dancing and I nearly nailed you in the elevator. You should kick me out, and make me sleep in the car."

He'd almost nailed her in the elevator? "Because why?"

His eyes closed for a beat. Obviously he was struggling with something. Maybe he didn't find her all that attractive now that she was undressed. But then he raised his lids and her breath stuttered at his visible anguish. "You're right. About what's really going on inside me, how I suppress passion, and I'm this close to losing control. You're so small. I don't want to hurt you. Scare you."

"Don't be ridiculous. You could never hurt me."

"Not intentionally." With a swallow, he said, "This should be like one of your fairy tales. I'm trying. I really am."

Her heart contracted, and she fell a little more. Somewhere in his whacked out creative mind, he'd come to the conclusion that romance equaled a chaste, *boring* encounter. He had missed the point.

She slid a hand under his shirt and placed it over his heart. With erratic beats pounding against her fingertips, she said, "Once upon a time, there was this prince who felt things so deeply, he was scared to let anyone else know, so he pretended he didn't feel anything at all. Then he met this princess who really got that. And she wishes he would get over it already and screw her brains out. The end."

He went still. Really still, and she nearly died. Kris being still was bad, especially now, at the watershed moment.

Come on, do it.

"I can't, VJ," he whispered. "You don't understand."

Her pulse leaped as she gave him the final push. "No. You don't understand. I want all of you. No holds barred. I can take whatever you've got. Really. Let go, Kristian."

Hunger whipped through his expression. Without warning,

he sat up, grinding against the naked flesh between her thighs as he captured her mouth possessively with his. Stars exploded in her head, at their joined lips.

She'd given him permission to let go. But she'd vastly underestimated what that meant.

It wasn't a kiss, but a primal mating call that swept through her veins like lava, demanding not only her body, but her soul. Long before the next beat of her heart, she surrendered.

Kris dropped the tight reins VJ had yanked from his fist. Just for now. Just this once.

His body howled, yearning to feel, snarling to charge ahead. The world ceased to exist.

He wrapped her hair, that seductive riot of curls, in his hand and tilted her head back to expose her neck, sucking and laving until she moaned, vibrating against his length. He throbbed in response.

"Yes," she whispered and rolled her hips against him, hot and fluid. "More. I'm so ready for you. What are you waiting for?"

He set her on her feet and stripped, ripping fabric and then fingering a condom into place. Impatiently, he hustled her backward until her back hit the wall. He crowded against her scorching body, skin on skin, a thigh between her legs and her slick center calling to him. The scent, sharp and feminine, saturated his senses.

Now. It had to be now. He lifted her leg and flung it around his waist. With both hands on her bottom, he boosted her higher on the wall and pierced her in one swift stroke.

Yes, finally.

He sucked in a breath, fighting to keep the explosion at bay as he filled her to the hilt. She stretched to accept him perfectly.

In her ear, he murmured in Greek and suddenly had the strangest urge to switch to English. "This is my favorite position," he said and withdrew so slowly, he thought he'd come apart. His voice was ragged. Raw. "You're so open. So deep."

English. Because he wanted her to understand him like no one else did.

As he pushed into her again, she stared him in the eye and said, "So are you."

Yeah. He was. She'd split him open with her beautiful honesty, and it wasn't terrible. There'd be a struggle to cram the lid back on, but that was later. Much later.

He slid out slowly to savor the feel of her. Too slow. He needed her, needed more, and she gave it instantly. *More.* And still more. She met him in the middle every time. So good. So amazing to just feel. To be lost in it. To give in to all the extremes, whatever they might be.

Harder and faster now, over and over, he pushed and she squirmed, as he wound them both higher with hard, insistent thrusts. She begged for more with that sexy moan. The wall kept her in place, steady, and the heat was intense, enveloping and surrounding him.

"I'm inside you," he said with his teeth on her earlobe. Her fingernails bit into his back in an unearthly mix of pain and pleasure. "Come for me."

With his name on her lips in a soul-shattering whisper, she did, clamping down on him so hard it triggered his own release. He poured himself out, eyes closed, muscles tensed, until he was so empty, he couldn't feel his bones. She'd taken everything and more, even parts he'd intended to keep.

Sweat-slicked chests heaving against each other, he let her slide down the length of his body until she'd gained her balance, then disposed of the condom and drew her over to the bed.

Drained, he lay next to her, face-to-face. Wincing, he fingered the side of her neck. When had he done that? "There's a bruise. I'm sorry. I didn't—"

"I'm not," she said. "Shut up and save your breath for round two, please. There are at least another hundred pages of the *Kama Sutra* left."

He laughed and enfolded her hand with his. All the shadowy guilt drained away. She was something else, with an inner strength he'd almost missed amid all her talk of romantic fantasies. "You're really amazing, you know that?"

"You, too." Her eyes were closed but the small smile on her face warmed him. "Let me know when you're rested up. The wall was hot and all, but I was pretty busy hanging on. I'd like to touch you. Here."

Before he could open his mouth to decline the tempting round-two offer, her fingers trailed down his abdomen and circled his length.

"Mmm," she purred. "You feel nice."

He swore as blood rushed from his head and half filled the flesh under her fingers. He should get out of the bed. Retreat before what little control he'd regained snapped for good. "So soon? Now I know you're overestimating my talents."

"Or you're underestimating mine." Both hands engulfed him and she rotated them in opposite directions, almost yanking another release from him.

This time the curse didn't make it out of his mouth. "Where did you learn that?"

"Auto-mechanic training." She smirked and with a sensuous slide of her body down his, was at his waist and taking him between her lips.

Too late. He couldn't leave now.

He didn't want to leave now.

Lost in the hot suction of her mouth, he shut his eyes. She moaned with him deep in her throat. Vibrations rocked him, his butt tightened and he came. Hard. Twice in one night.

Victoria Jane was going to renew his faith.

"I'm in awe," he murmured when she settled up against him. "You do have talent."

"I've never done it before. Did I do it right?" She buried her face in his shoulder.

She was such a hot mix of seductress and innocent. Everything about her was arousing. He bit back a smile. "Maybe you should try again. Practice makes perfect."

She smacked him, and he did laugh then. "I told you this would be fun," he said. "I can't remember it ever being this good."

"That's because you've always been so focused on pretending you're unaffected. It takes a lot of energy to hold back." She flipped onto her stomach and spread one of those gorgeous hands on his chest. She rested her chin on her fingers and sought his gaze. "Don't do that anymore. Not with me."

"But it's okay with other women?"

She screwed up her face adorably. "Yep. Definitely hold back with other women. Actually, I'd recommend not having sex with anyone besides me ever again."

Adorable and dangerous. Dangerously addicting. She was upfront about everything, including her predictable desire for monogamy, and transparency turned him on. "I'll stick with you for now. Hungry yet?"

"I could eat. You gonna buy me dinner after I've already put out?" She sighed lustily. "Now I know I'm not in Texas anymore."

He pulled her up and kissed her sexy swollen lips. "Get dressed. But not in that." He flipped a hand at his favorite dress in the whole world. "Something that covers you or you'll starve before I let you out of this bedroom."

"Um, don't they have room service?" She arched a brow suggestively. "I remember this guy with a cart."

"Beauty and brains. Have I told you lately how much I like you?"

She grinned and straddled him. "Give me five minutes. Then you can tell me again," she said, and rubbed her slick, naked sex all over his, eliciting a groan from deep in his chest as his groin sprang to life.

"I'll be drowning in you in five minutes."

She took him in her blistering hands, fumbled endearingly with a condom and guided him to her entrance. Just before she impaled herself, she whispered, "I know mouth-to-mouth," and kissed him, tongue hot against his. She slid up and down with slow, tight strokes. His eyes nearly rolled back in his head and garbled words caught in his throat.

"I'm not hurting you, am I?" she asked and paused, concern plastered across her expression. "Or scaring you?"

"No way. Don't stop. Please," he slurred and then saw the furtive smile she couldn't hide. "Oh, you're hilarious. I'm over it, okay? You win by a landslide. Hope that compensates for not getting your fairy tale."

"Kris." She leaned back to peer at him, driving him deeper and nearly killing him. "You're here. That's the fairy tale. Not the setting or the words or the rose petals. All it takes for this to be magic is you."

And then she pushed down even harder, nipped his chest with her fingernails and turned herself into a complete liar because the magic was in her touch. A spell was the only explanation for why he was still engaged, still desperate for her.

It did take a lot of energy to hold back. He'd just never been able to let go before. Never wanted to.

An eternity later, she finally admitted to being too sore to do anything other than eat. They ordered something to be delivered to the room, and whatever it was, he ate it while watching VJ as she entertained him with stories about small town life. She had a glow so strong and beautiful, the camera would pick it up easily, and he had a possessive sense of pride for being responsible.

He also had a responsibility to end this thing quickly. Passion this strong would fade faster than normal, and he was terrified of what would happen when it did. He had no intention of sticking around to find out.

After both plates were clear, she yawned. "Thank you for the wonderful birthday. It was the best present ever. I'm afraid I'm about to crash. Is this the part where we say good-night?"

"Absolutely not." The force of his denial surprised him since he'd been about to send her off to her room. Where had that come from? Sleeping alone was habitual. Necessary. Lonely. "Forget about the other bedroom. Get your things. Move them. That door is off-limits." He thrust a finger at the offending door. "I want to watch you fall asleep in my arms."

Yeah. He did. Just until he went back to L.A. This whatever-it-was with VJ had blossomed into more than he'd been prepared for but with the promise of escape at the end of the week, he could handle it for a few days. It wasn't like moving in together, which he'd never tried with anyone.

"Okay. If you insist." She smiled, and it was treacherous. "I did want to try one other position. In the morning. You know, spoon style. Unless you want to try it now?"

On cue, the shoulder of the bathrobe fell to her elbow.

Ten

At dawn, Kris drew the drapes from the bedroom window and settled back in bed to watch the colors of the sunrise bleed into the indigo above the Dallas skyline. VJ woke long enough to snuggle up and then fell back asleep with her tousled head in the hollow of his shoulder. It was disconcerting how easily she fit and how easily he suspected he could get used to it.

He couldn't remember the last time he'd watched the night disappear into day. Small, restive pleasures were a luxury he'd forgotten in the rush of everyday life. Normally, he was out of bed and doing stuff by now. Restlessness VJ called it, and somehow, she'd tamed it. With a warm and willing woman in his bed, it hadn't seemed so important to bolt into the chaos yet.

Plus, he was stalling.

At 8:03 a.m., Kris eased out from under VJ's head and placed it carefully on the pillow. She sighed and flipped over onto her back, pulling the sheet down to her stomach and exposing that gorgeous butterfly. Small bruises dotted her neck and discolored the fragile tissue of her breasts. Guilt ate at him.

Then he remembered. She could take it. Wanted it. Begged for it. He nearly crawled back in to indulge in sleepy, morning sex. Spoon style.

But he didn't.

Out in the living area, he found his phone on the coffee table and flipped to the *M's*, then hit Call. It rang eight times. On the ninth ring, Kyla finally answered.

"Hey," she said and barely sounded hung over at all. World-class acting even without the camera in front of her.

"Hey." He paused, weighing how to approach the subject of VJ. With Kyla, nothing was simple. "Sorry. It's important or I would have waited."

"I'm still in bed, babe. Nothing's that important. Unless you're coming over to join me?" The hopefulness in her voice crawled on his last nerve and raked it raw.

"I met someone."

And that's what happened when he let Kyla rile him. He blurted out stuff he shouldn't. A loud clatter greeted the announcement, which was better than the cursing he'd expected.

"Okay," she said. "I'm sitting up. So that's why it took you so long to call. Can you give me a minute to find some coffee before you throw something like that on me?"

A few simple words and suddenly, the situation teetered on the edge of becoming a huge problem. Kyla did not like that he'd met "someone." "Listen, Kyla. I'm not going to do the fake engagement. I can't. I never liked the idea."

She was quiet for a minute and then exhaled in a long stream, likely smoking the first cigarette of her two packs a day. "Have you told Jack Abrams yet?"

Of course that was her first question. Digging, to find out how far he'd taken it. "Don't worry. You still have a job."

"I'm not worried about me. I'm worried about you, darling. Have you thought this through?"

"Yes, I have." He gritted his teeth before he called her a liar. She never worried about anyone other than herself.

"Then what's the plan? The contracts are signed. Did you bring in someone else to deal with the publicity and advertising?"

His back teeth scraped together. No. But he should have thought of it. Should have secured an additional investor before bringing this up with someone as savvy as Kyla.

He hadn't because VJ deserved to have these ties severed before he slept with her again. Really, it should have happened before last night, but then he'd been sure last night would end in separate bedrooms. When it hadn't, he'd been a little too busy to pick up the phone.

"I'm still working on the alternative plan. Do you want your car? I'll drop it off to you today."

"Guy's having a thing tonight at Club 47. Bring the car by." He did not like the crafty note creeping into her tone. "And your new friend. I'd like to meet her."

Yeah. That was going to happen. He sank down on the couch, unsure if he'd get through this without breaking something. VJ had uncorked the fire and reclosing the lid on his soul sucked. But he had to find a balance. "We're busy. I'll bring the car to your mother's around three."

"Now you've got me curious. Who is she?"

"No one you'd know."

"She must be dog ugly."

"For Christ—" He was up and pacing before he realized it. "You're unbelievable."

"And you can't still be upset about Guy. We're just friends now."

As he'd suspected. She and Guy had split up, and she'd had her sights set on Kris again.

"I'm not upset about Guy."

"Come to the club. It'll be fun. Show your new friend a good time."

He could think of a hundred things he and VJ could do for

fun besides spending the evening in a pit of vipers. "She's not my friend."

"Oh, my God. It's that serious? Is *she* the reason you don't want to do the engagement? You made it sound like—"

"Kyla. Stop." Now he had to go to the party. If nothing else, to prove to Kyla he wasn't serious about VJ. "We'll be there to drop off the car and kill your curiosity. We won't stay."

His and VJ's relationship had a short life—very short—and that wasn't going to change regardless of what Kyla said to bait him. The engagement was incidental to his feelings about VJ. He liked her, and they had fun. It wasn't as if he'd subconsciously sought to remove the Kyla obstacle in case this thing with VJ progressed.

This thing with VJ *couldn't* progress.

He needed to back off again. The more he practiced reattaching that lid, the easier it would be to do it permanently.

He ended the call and got lost in work instead of VJ, but wondered the whole time why it bothered him. Why the ache in his chest wouldn't ease no matter what he did.

When VJ woke—alone— she cocked an ear for the sound of the shower, but the bathroom door stood ajar and the interior was dark. She sat up and was immediately sorry. Everything hurt. But deliciously, rightly so. Last night had bordered on mythical.

She flopped back on the pillow and grinned at the ceiling. This bed still belonged to Kris even if he wasn't in it. She'd slept sinfully late and he was a busy man, who had spent the entire day with her yesterday. He probably needed to catch up on work and if she left him alone, maybe she'd get some of his time later.

She limped into the bathroom, beamed at the marks Kris had trailed down her throat and threw on a robe. She wandered out of the bedroom. Kris sat at the table chained to his laptop. Morning light spilled through the bay window, cloaking him in an ethereal spotlight. He glanced up, hair falling in his face and that slow smile knocked her knees loose. How had he picked her out of all the other mortals available?

"Come here," he said.

As she crossed to him, he slapped the computer closed, shoved the chair back a foot and pulled her into his lap. Then kissed her. Thoroughly.

If he did that every morning for the rest of her life, it wouldn't be enough. "Um, wow. Good morning to you, too," she said when his lips lifted.

Instead of responding, he slid his hands up her arms and hooked the robe's lapels, drawing them off her shoulders to bare her breasts. He traced a lazy pattern down her neck and circled both nipples until she was nearly panting with need.

He sighed, kissed the butterfly and covered her up again. "I have to do some things today. But I'm taking you out tonight. Will you be okay on your own until about five?"

"Sure." She swallowed and pressed her legs together until the heat subsided through sheer will alone. "I assumed you'd be working anyway. What are we doing tonight?"

"I'll tell you later. Happy birthday."

Her heart skipped. Mama had been the only one who'd ever remembered at home. "Thanks."

"Okay, now go away so I can concentrate." He grinned and pushed her lightly. She left him to his work, with only one backward glance at his pursed lips. The things that mouth could do. Shudder and a half.

She went to the pool and started rereading *Embrace the Rogue* for the four hundredth time. Even her favorite book couldn't hold her interest, so she put it down and closed her eyes, drifting in the hot sun amidst the shrieks of kids splashing in the shallow end. She ate lunch by herself and missed Kris so badly she ached. At four o'clock, hot and sweaty, she went back to the room.

Empty. Kris's laptop was on the table, closed, but he was gone and his phone wasn't on the coffee table.

Well, he didn't answer to her. He'd be back eventually.

Kris had been clear about not using her bedroom so she flipped on the water in his shower and tossed her swimsuit into the corner. As she swung open the shower door to step into the tepid spray, Kris strolled into the bathroom, his grin extremely decadent.

"Exactly where I hoped I'd find you," he said and started undressing as if it was perfectly natural to be in the bathroom with her—naked—at the same time. Her cheeks heated, inexplicably. She couldn't possibly still be shy after last night. Could she?

Her tongue was suddenly too big for her mouth, and she couldn't speak as his shirt came off, then his pants. His boxer briefs clung to his thighs—and why was he taking so long to get them off?

Then he was naked, and he was beautiful. Every smooth, golden limb and whorl of hair on his chest was exquisite. Gorgeous.

He enfolded her in his arms and held her for a moment, hands curved around her back, warm against her skin. Held her, as if cradling something precious and treasured. Embracing her intimately, instead of diving right into hot sex. His touch carried sweet nuances of all his unexpressed feelings. *Yes, yes, yes.* Last night had fundamentally changed their relationship.

Her stomach, then her heart flipped. Holy macaroni, she was so far gone over him.

"Where were we?" he murmured and nuzzled her neck.

"Um, Dallas?"

He laughed and pulled the handle on the glass shower door. "Get wet. I want to make you scream as I'm soaping you up."

Hot waves skewered her, and she almost came right then. How did he do that with just his voice?

He swept her into the shower and spun her, pushing her up

against the tiles, then pressed her flat with his hard body while whispering in her ear. The freezing tiles against her breasts and stomach combined with the heat of him on her back sent a barb through her womb. She'd unleashed a monster, and the power of it nearly finished the orgasm his voice had started.

His lathered hands slid along her sides, scandalously dipping into the crevice of her bottom, but it was luscious and she arched, seeking him, wanting him. His fingers twisted into her center with lovely friction, and she moaned.

"That's right," he murmured. "Tell me how much you like it."

He was checking in. Even after everything she'd done last night, he wanted to be sure she was still okay with no-holds-barred. Subtly asking her for reassurance before he did something irreversible. How could she do anything but fall for him?

"You make me so hot. Feels so good," she said hoarsely, and moaned his name as he teased her with sensuous circles. Sparks gathered and the tightness grew. "I need you now."

He drew her leg up, and positioned her foot on the low shelf, guided her forward and plowed into her. Yes, so good.

"More," she cried. "Faster."

And he did both. She writhed as he touched her everywhere. Then he did something indescribable against her sex as he slid deep, scraping his hard teeth against the hollow of her collarbone. She came in a whirlpool of thick sensation with a half scream.

"Yes. Beautiful," he said fiercely, and held her firm against his chest as she climaxed again and again, lost in a delirium of pleasure. Her vision blurred.

When she could see again, she was still locked in his embrace, water sluicing over her, and he was stroking wet hair out of her face.

"You're so gorgeous when you come," he said, his lips grazing her ear. "So uninhibited. I want you again just thinking about it."

She turned in his arms and took his mouth in a hard, desperate kiss, then shoved him backward until he collapsed on the shelf. She mounted him. "You can see me better from this angle."

His expression turned feral. "You're insatiable. I can't tell you how much I like that."

Circling his hips against hers, rubbing their bodies together carnally, he sparked a mad fire, enflaming her deep at the core. She needed him, craved him. Never had she felt this kind of drive to be with someone. Only Kris.

The monster *had* been unleashed but it was inside her. All her feelings for this man had exploded from their bonds, seeking to claim even as she was claimed. She barely understood the ways he made her whole, made her more than what she'd been. Barely understood the drive to reach completion again and again.

She'd been waiting for this, for him, her entire life.

As he drove her higher, faster, fiercer and longer than the first time, as she was about to drop off that ledge and free fall into climax, she found his gaze and stared into his open eyes as she shattered.

He shuddered with his own release but didn't break their locked gazes, and the emotion in his melty eyes—affection, pleasure, affinity—squeezed her heart. Squeezed so hard, tears formed. One slid down her face, and in the aftermath, still joined and totally overcome, she mouthed *I love you*.

Shock darted through his expression. She cursed. She hadn't meant for him to hear her.

She stood and backed away, taking measured breaths to calm her racing pulse. "Sorry, heat of the moment. Don't worry, it's not contagious."

His eyes turned flat and unreadable. Inaccessible Kristian Demetrious had returned.

"Come back and let me finish washing you," he said.

Eyes narrowed, she did, but when he touched her, it was

impersonal. Great. How in the world would she counteract this disaster?

The atmosphere was strained for the remainder of their shower and as they got dressed. He talked to her. She talked back, but couldn't find the groove where they were intimate with each other. They shared the bathroom sink and mirror, accidentally touched, did a hundred other things that a real couple might but it wasn't right. Panic erupted like a swarm of angry monarchs flying down her windpipe and she couldn't get her eyeliner straight.

They went to dinner at a different place than last night and she had no illusions about whether they would eat this time. Halfway through the salad course, she put her fork down. "Can we talk about it?"

"Talk about what?" He twirled the fork in his fingers and caught it, then stabbed some lettuce as if it had tried to get up and walk off his plate.

"You know what. The shower."

"I'm partial to showers, myself. Aren't you?"

Resorting to deflection. Why was she not surprised? "I say that to all the guys I'm sleeping with. Don't read into it."

His face froze. He picked up his wineglass and sat back in the chair, all pretense of eating gone. "Well, I feel special."

What kind of response was that? Suddenly she was tired of trying to burrow through, under or around that wall. Tired of waiting for that moment when it would all come together.

She buried her face in her hands and willed back the sudden urge to stand and run. "What do you expect me to say? That you're nothing to me, and I can't wait to ditch you? That I don't have any feelings for you? I can't. Both would be as much a lie as telling you I say that to all the guys. Guy. There's only been one other."

"Look at me."

She raised her head. With a small smile, he held out a hand, palm up. Cautiously, she placed her hand in his and he squeezed it tight. She braced.

Here it comes. It's not you, it's me.

"You're the most fascinating and exciting woman I've ever met," he said. "The most attractive part is your honesty. I have to accept that sometimes it might lead to a little more honesty than expected. If that's how you feel, I appreciate that you trust me enough to say so. I'm sorry I didn't handle it well. You took me by surprise. That's all."

"Did you just apologize to me?" Her throat wasn't working right, and it was going to be a close call whether or not she cried. Kris thought she was fascinating and exciting. Instead of continuing to freak out over her slip, he'd apologized. This was way better than a romance novel.

"I did, because I was acting badly. So I'll do it again. I'm sorry. I don't want to spend the rest of our time together being at odds. We've only got a few days before I go back to L.A."

A few days? Back to L.A.?

When had English become her second language?

"Can we put it behind us and have a good time tonight?" he asked and stroked her knuckle.

"Sure." Somewhere she'd lost the thread of the conversation and desperately, she cast about, trying to grasp it again. "What's on the agenda for the evening?"

"A get-together with some people I know."

"Sounds fun. Oh, look, here's dinner."

Gratefully, she released his hand and sat back to give the waiter access. She picked up her fork and dug into the main course, with no idea what it was.

Kris was still planning to end it with her and leave in a few days. Instead of breaking down his barriers, she'd screwed up and added one more. Whatever progress she'd made had been thoroughly erased the moment she dropped the *L* word.

Grief pulled at her mouth. She was waiting in vain for the moment when things would come together because her math skills clearly left a lot to be desired. None of this was working. He'd opened up and all that amazing passion discharged like a crackle of lightning, just as she'd known it would. But it was strictly one-way. A release of energy, not a significant encounter that caused him to reevaluate.

As soon as the waiter was out of earshot, she fell back on the tried-and-true method to regain her equilibrium. If he wanted fun, fun he'd get, at least until she figured out how to turn one and one into two. "What's the wildest place you've ever had sex?"

He grinned and the tension was gone, at least as far as he knew. It was still there, across the back of her neck and racing through her mind as she tried to reconcile the very different agendas playing out on the field of their relationship.

"You mean someplace other than in the shower with you earlier?" His fork disappeared into his mouth.

She had bricks in her chest and he was eating.

"Yeah, that doesn't count."

"Sorry, that was so good, it erased my memory. Can I tell you how unbelievably hot it is that you're ready to go again within minutes?"

"It's all in the wrist."

He was being purposely evasive, too much the gentleman to flaunt his experience with other women. Of course it made her love him that much more. How could they be on such different pages?

"What about you?" he asked with a lifted chin. "Other than the shower. Wildest place."

"The couch."

He toasted her with his wineglass. "We'll have to remedy that. Pick a place. Any place. I find myself fond of being your guinea pig."

"Hood of the car." Really, she couldn't even think about this now.

He winced. "You mean the Ferrari?"

She raised an eyebrow. "You got another one?"

"The Ferrari belongs to Kyla. I'm dropping it off to her tonight, so maybe you should pick another place. Why are you grinning like that?"

The Ferrari wasn't Kris's. The thought thrilled her. The final piece of the puzzle clicked into place—the engine inside his head wasn't complex and foreign after all. She *knew* Kristian Demetrious, and therefore, she knew better than to believe the lies he told himself. He was falling back on old habits of denying his feelings because…well, she didn't know exactly why he did it but that didn't change the facts. She hadn't misread him or tripped up by confessing her feelings.

He thought he was leaving in a few days. And she was going to change his mind.

One more big push, and he'd never leave her because he would realize they were meant to be together forever.

Eleven

The driving beat, audible even outside the club, thumped against VJ's ribs as Kris led her past the crowd lined up between red ropes and to an unmarked door around the side.

"Secret VIP entrance?" she asked.

"Something like that."

Kris nodded to the doorman, who pushed open the door, and Kris took her hand as she crossed the threshold into another world of thick smoke and strafing lights. People were everywhere, three deep at the bar, crushed together on the dance floor. All of them reeked of money.

"Am I allowed to be a little starstruck?" she shouted over the music and tightened her grip on Kris's hand so she couldn't fiddle with her hair or dress again. No one was going to notice her anyway, not with a Greek god casting her into shadow.

"No. They're just people," he said shortly.

All his answers had been short since they'd gotten into the car after dinner, including when he told her Kyla would be at the club and yes, it would be awkward. Unfortunately, so far, he'd been the one making it awkward with his odd aloofness. Inaccessible Kristian Demetrious was not her favorite companion.

Thankfully she'd worn the black dress last night so she could wear the red one tonight. It was calf-length with a Jezebel slit up the center. All the way up. Any higher and she'd be arrested for indecency. Dozens of glittery straps zigzagged across her bust and torso, then around to her back, allowing a lot of bare skin to peek through. All she needed now was the devil's pitchfork and some horns, but at least she looked her best and it bolstered her confidence.

Another hulking bouncer guarded the ropes leading to some steps and nodded to Kris when they approached. He unhooked the catch and stepped aside. The result of Kris being famous or because he'd been here before? Maybe it was because he radiated a sense of authority wherever he went.

At the top of the stairs, another room overlooked the main dance floor. This was clearly the place to be. The people below didn't reek of money. She'd been mistaken. They reeked of pretense, and there was no comparison. *These* people had wealth, class and prestige that poured off of them in waves. Just like Kris.

Her eyes darted everywhere, taking in the diamonds and European cigarettes along with the faces of celebrities often seen in magazines and on TV. The music was quieter here as if fame had a dampening effect on acoustics.

"Is that a Jonas brother?" she couldn't help but ask and then bit her tongue. She was going to embarrass herself and Kris if she didn't shut up, but she was still off balance from dinner.

Kris smiled without humor and pulled her into the sea of superstars.

Kyla Monroe was ringed by a throng of admirers, a modern-day Scarlett O'Hara in Scarlett Johansson's body. In person, she looked the same as she did on the screen. Perfect. Every platinum hair in place, flawless makeup, unblemished skin. She must carry a salon in her clutch that beautified by osmosis.

VJ's stomach clenched. They'd both slept with the same man. Kris had touched Kyla the same way he'd touched her and probably a lot more times. He'd learned how to do that sucking thing with his mouth from somewhere. Scorpions scuttling along her spine—that's what it felt like to step into the same room as his ex-girlfriend. His beautiful, poised, glamorous ex-girlfriend.

How did people in Hollywood do this?

Like this.

With confidence drawn from who-knew-where, she pasted on a smile and strode forward to take Kyla's manicured hand. These were the people Kris interacted with every day, and she'd fit in or be crucified. If it was the latter, at least she'd be dead.

"So this is your new friend." Kyla's eyes cut over VJ smoothly. "Kris forgot to mention how striking you are. Catch me before you leave, and I'll give you my agent's number. You should call him. I'll put in a good word for you."

"She's not interested," Kris answered for her, fortunately, since she was speechless.

"I'm interested." A breathtakingly stunning male of the blond Nordic variety had materialized at Kyla's side. "Introduce us, why don't you?"

VJ almost fainted when she recognized him.

"VJ Lewis," Kris said icily. "This is Guy Hansen."

"I've seen all your movies," VJ gushed as she shook his hand. "I loved the last one about the runaway train. Very edge-of-your-seat."

"Ah, the magic of editing." Guy hadn't released her hand yet, and he didn't until Kris pulled her away and tucked her underneath his arm.

The glower on Kris's face could have cooked bacon. VJ did a double take. Jealousy. Because she'd seen Guy's movies but not Kris's? Well, it wasn't her fault the Cineplex in Van Horn played blow-'em-up action movies starring actors with six-pack abs and didn't show independent films.

Lacing fingers with Kris, she leaned in so only he could hear. "It's too bad he's so ugly. Think how successful he could be with a little plastic surgery. Although, he doesn't speak Greek, so he'll never be perfect."

Kris kissed her temple and his lips lingered for an intimate beat. Kyla didn't miss it. As she glanced back and forth between VJ and Kris, her eyes glittered against the colored strobe lights behind her.

"Babe, run get us some drinks. I'd like to talk to VJ." Kyla ran a proprietary hand down Kris's arm and smiled at VJ like the lead in a toothpaste commercial. "He knows what I drink. What would you like?"

VJ smiled at Kyla like the lead in a vampire movie and said, "He knows what I drink, too. And how I take my eggs in the morning."

Guy whistled. "Look out."

Kyla laughed and pushed both men aside. "Go. Both of you. Girl talk will only make you vomit."

VJ shooed Kris off. "It's okay. I'll be fine," she whispered.

Kris backed away, his aura full of sharp angles and his mouth hard. He didn't take his eyes off either woman as he flagged down a harried cocktail waitress.

"You're not at all what I expected," Kyla said, once Kris was out of earshot. "But I can see why Kris likes you."

Kris liked her because she understood him better than anyone on Earth and enabled him be the real person he was inside.

But, a glimpse into the psyche of the man VJ loved via his ex was too tempting to pass up.

"Really? Why?"

"You don't take any crap. He likes strong women who take care of themselves. What do you do?"

Kris liked strong women. Who took care of themselves.

So far, she hadn't been racking up too many points on either count. "What do I do about what?"

"For your career." Kyla sat gracefully on one of the leather couches lining the wall of the club and crossed her legs in a way too posed to be comfortable, but which showed off her toned thighs. It was astonishing how she'd done that without falling to the floor.

"I'm between engagements. Considering my options."

The last thing she'd admit to this accomplished woman was how bleak prospects were for eating next week, never mind the luxury of choosing a career.

"Good for you. Very smart to consider all the options." Kyla swept her with another full-length glance as VJ joined her on the couch. "I love that dress. Roberto Cavalli is one of my favorite designers."

"Thanks." There was no way she could reciprocate. She had no idea who'd designed the stunning sequined dress Kyla was wearing and probably wouldn't know how to pronounce it if she did. And she had a feeling Kyla was leading up to something. Nerves kicked at her, and she wedged her hands under her skirt.

"Can I ask you something?" Kyla went on without pausing. "Did Kris tell you about the financing for his next movie?"

"Of course. He doesn't keep secrets from me."

A cigarette appeared between Kyla's fingers and she waved off Guy who'd returned and jumped over with a light. "Then you must know the film's budget is tied to the publicity campaign Kris just threw in the trash. He must care about you a great deal to give up that film."

The flame from Kyla's lighter mesmerized VJ for a moment, and she didn't immediately register what the other woman had said. "What?"

"Oops." Kyla flinched and with a laugh, shook her head. "I assumed you knew the deal with Jack Abrams fell through since you don't have any secrets."

"Fell through? No, Kris is working on alternatives. He told me."

Though she and Kyla were almost the same age, the sudden shrewd light in the other woman's eyes said VJ was young and naive.

"Making movies is about money and ego, and when money and ego are involved, so are contracts. Directors don't have the luxury of alternatives, no matter what Kris told you. Oh, I hope I didn't cause problems between the two of you. He deserves to be happy. Speak of the devil." Kyla nodded with a raised brow as Kris crossed the room with two drinks in hand. The VIP section wasn't nearly dim enough to hide his back-off vibe, which she suspected he radiated reflexively when around other people.

"Enough girl talk." Kris handed Kyla her drink. He extended the same hand to VJ, pulled her off the couch and positioned a stiff arm around her waist. "VJ and I will finish our drinks elsewhere and then we're leaving. Hansen has the valet claim ticket for your car. I'll call you later about meeting with the studio."

"I was doing all right," VJ said as he guided her across the room. "I would have rescued myself if I wasn't."

"I shouldn't have left you with her, but you insisted. I should have said no." Kris downed his drink in one shot, lights bouncing off the shiny glass as he tilted it back. She'd never seen him drink so much. She wouldn't have noticed except for his weird mood, which was getting harder to blame on being in public instead of the more likely cause—he might be okay with honesty, but not with her loving him.

"Kyla was nice."

Kris snorted. "Nice for a cobra. At least once she poisons you, death is quick. What did she say?"

"She complimented my dress and said you deserve to be happy. Which is true."

She should mention the film. She should ask him what was going to happen now that he'd called off the engagement. Naively, she'd assumed it would all work out, and Kris would still get to make his movie in spite of having met her.

Her drink disappeared in a few gulps, but it didn't loosen her tongue.

Kris glanced at his phone and motioned toward the door. "Ready?"

Now was her chance to ask if he was really giving up the film for her. If he was sacrificing something he couldn't afford to lose this time, instead of giving up something he wasn't using anyway. Then maybe he'd admit he was in love with her, sweep her into his arms and announce that no mere movie could compare with the depths of completion VJ brought him. He would confess he'd been acting weird because he didn't know how to handle his emotions.

It could happen.

A tremor stopped her words cold. Music pounded through the sudden hollowness of her chest. He'd spent the last four days telling her how important this movie was and how his entire career hinged on it. Every second he wasn't with her or sleeping, he clacked away on his laptop, dealing with Important Director Matters. Kyla mentioned contracts, which meant legal entanglements she'd never even considered.

She couldn't let him give up the movie. For any reason.

So, either Kris was going back to L.A. in a few days to make his movie like he'd said at dinner, and she'd not only have to accept it, she'd have to encourage him to do the engagement after all. Or it was already too late and she'd ruined everything.

The last option, the one where Kris ended up with her *and* the movie, fell into a distant, highly implausible third place.

Suddenly, she didn't want to know which one it was. Not tonight. Tomorrow was soon enough to ask.

They'd left the club hours ago and Kris still couldn't banish the edgy scrabbling at the back of his neck. Awake and restless, he stared through the open drapes at the dark skyline and pulled VJ's sleeping form a little closer, though she was already almost on top of him. It was never close enough, especially not after exposing her to Kyla and the person he always became around her. VJ cleansed all that from his system.

His plan to take her to the club to solidify the temporary nature of his relationship with VJ hadn't worked. The part where he'd tried to back off again hadn't worked, either. All night, he'd carried a sharp, underlying awareness that VJ was in love with him.

Clearly, they defined the words *fun* and *temporary* differently, or she'd never been on board with either from the beginning, which was the most likely. He'd known better than to get involved, but hadn't been able to resist. Then, when she did exactly as he'd come to expect—said what was in her heart—he acted surprised. His bone-headedness in the shower had been driven purely by the ache in his throat from not being able to say it back.

He'd never said that to anyone, never even come close. Never thought for a moment what he felt might be love. Until now.

VJ made it easy to feel. Necessary to feel. She was in love with him, and the knowledge settled inside with a heavy, unique relevance. Honestly, he'd been eager to leave the club and be alone with her. He'd never cared about that before. Hollywood parties were endless and he usually left unaccompanied. How had this whatever-it-was with VJ progressed this far?

VJ sighed softly and burrowed her head into his shoulder a little deeper. He breathed in the wave of sweetness from her hair, hair he'd washed with his own hands.

The emotionally heavy tang of her on his skin, with that cinnamon hair splayed across his chest as she slept naked in his bed, unearthed a fierce longing in his gut to grab on to her and never let go. To maintain this cocoon she created around the two of them. When he was inside it, anything and everything was possible. *That's* how it had progressed this far.

If anyone could make him believe in fairy tales, she could.

He threaded that amazing hair through his fingers and cupped her face, gently kissing her awake because he had to. She was a persistence of vision he couldn't erase. She stirred and rolled with a tiny wiggle until they were snugged tight with her rounded bottom against his hips. Drowsily, she steered his palm to her breast and murmured, "Need you, Kristian. Love me."

In an instant, he sank into her. Tight inside her, inside that dreamlike state that was somehow reality and he fell into it closefisted. Prolonged it as long as he could. VJ arched against his chest in a beautiful bow and tangled her legs with his, thrusting him deep and tunneling under his skin with her soft sigh.

At the moment he fractured, the theme for *Visions of Black* came to him on a spur of inspiration. It was so brilliant and obvious. How had he missed it?

VJ collapsed into the pillow and fell asleep wrapped firmly in his arms. His brain clicked into high gear with lighting angles, set pieces, script changes. But he couldn't give up holding VJ just yet. Soon, he wouldn't have a choice but to give her up. His life didn't have a fairy-tale ending and he'd be selfish to continue down this spiral when he couldn't promise her anything past the next few days.

The longer he spent with her, the wider she'd crack him open and the harder it would be to keep the lid in place. The harder it would be to control the darkness he knew lived inside, lurking, waiting to turn something beautiful into ugliness.

At dawn he crawled out of bed. Work beckoned. And he needed some time away from VJ or he'd never regain his balance.

As soon as his laptop booted up, he typed a ton of notes. *Visions of Black* had two elements: the full-color, disjointed visions and the black-and-white hospital scenes, which represented the main character's reality of blindness and amnesia. He'd been stumbling over it, but in his moment of clarity, he'd realized the visions were her reality and the hospital the altered state. That's why it hadn't been working. Once he flipped them, everything came together. The theme was altered reality.

After a couple of hours, he'd finished pouring the contents of his brain onto the page. Next, he opened the Creative Financing file and added the idea he'd come up with a few minutes ago. *Borrow against future gross.* Which was not great, because it granted rights to profit on a film he hadn't even conceptualized yet, but it beat the fake engagement.

The other ideas weren't stellar, either. He rubbed his eyes and blinked at the screen. None of this would net the backing he needed to make a blockbuster of *Visions of Black*. Guys starting out did this kind of scrambling, stuff he'd done ten years ago to put enough money in his hands to commit brilliance to film and impress the deep pockets into taking a chance on him.

And finally, after years of bleeding his emotional center onto the screen, one of those deep pockets stepped forward. Jack Abrams signed on the dotted line, but to compensate for Kyla's exorbitant salary, Kris had agreed to cut advertising dollars and stir up publicity with the engagement. It had seemed like a fair trade at the time.

Studios were evil. But they had connections, distribution channels, promotional departments. Things an independent film director only dreamed of.

Kris made coffee and waited until the brewer trickled the final drop into the pot before pulling out his phone to call Jack Abrams. He'd put off the call, hoping a genius idea for promoting *Visions of Black* would fall from the sky.

The hour was still early on the west coast but Jack was a morning person, too. Kris hoped their good working relationship would smooth out the issues from the bomb he was about to drop.

"Mr. Abrams," he said when the other man answered. "It's Kris Demetrious. Sorry to bother you, but I need to tell you I've decided not to announce my engagement to Kyla Monroe."

"Not announcing it?" Jack paused. "Or not going through with it at all?"

"Not going through with it at all," Kris said. "It's not the right path. I'd like to discuss other options."

"I'm a little taken aback," Jack said gruffly. "We all agreed on this publicity angle."

"Yes, sir. I changed my mind. I'd like to renegotiate funds for advertising instead."

"That's not possible. The numbers are the numbers and our contract is solid." Jack Abrams was a powerful man and the nuances of his statement weren't lost on Kris.

"I understand. I intend to honor the contract. I'm asking you to be open to other possibilities."

"I wouldn't be opposed to reallocating."

Which meant Kris would have to cut somewhere else, but the budget was too tight for that. Kyla's salary was the major sticking point. She was a huge draw, and she'd already approved the script. Above all, the role needed her particular spin. No other actress would be right. He couldn't shoot the movie without her. "Thank you, sir. I don't think that will work."

"Then it doesn't sound as if you have a choice but to stick with the original plan."

"No, sir. It doesn't."

Kris ended the call and contemplated smashing his phone through the laptop screen. But he needed it to call Kyla and talk her into taking less money. That conversation didn't go any better. She refused to listen and instead issued a thinly veiled threat to speak to her lawyer if he didn't get with the program. So much for hoping their history might sway her toward a peaceable solution.

His temples throbbed. Years of work, about to go down the drain because he couldn't pretend to be engaged to Kyla. Yes, he'd agreed to it. But that had been before VJ put his cynicism through the shredder and spliced his psyche back together into something he didn't fully understand yet. But he did know people should see *Visions* because he'd created something brilliant, not because of a fictitious engagement.

He had no choice but to find another way. He would not be forced to cool things off with VJ to make an engagement to Kyla believable, all because Abrams and Kyla refused to budge. The cool-off would happen when and how he decided. Hollywood did not control his life.

Disgusted, he stabbed the power button on the TV remote. He hated TV. The chances of finding a decent enough distraction were about zero but he flipped through the channels anyway, hoping to stumble over an old Hitchcock or Kubrick flick.

Photos of him and VJ leaving the club last night, as well as ones from the restaurant the night they didn't eat, crowded the screen of a national morning talk show.

"Wow. That dress photographs well." VJ plopped down on the couch next to him and kissed his shoulder.

His black mood lightened as she tucked her legs up under the robe and leaned against him. He turned up the sound, curious how the two of them were news, just as the still shot dissolved into one of Kyla.

"…statement from her publicist, box-office sweetheart Kyla Monroe confirms her relationship with director Kristian Demetrious has ended," the reporter said. "Unconfirmed speculation names the unidentified woman in these photos as the cause."

"What is she talking about?" VJ glanced at Kris.

"I have no idea." He shrugged.

"Well, your relationship with Kyla is over. At least they got that part right. But it was over a while ago." Her tongue came out to lick her lips. "Right?"

Not this on top of the conversations with Abrams and Kyla and *you have no choice* still ringing in his ears. His temper veered back to bad. "Kyla and I broke up a few months ago, but she asked me not to issue a statement and I didn't. Thanks for the trust."

"I'm sorry. We've never actually talked about it." She

rubbed his shoulder and cleared her throat. "Speaking of which. There's something else we really need to get straight. The promotion for your movie. Kyla said a few things last night that didn't make sense."

Great. First VJ accused him of playing two women at once, and now she wanted to hash out wisdom from the mouth of Kyla. "Kyla says lots of stuff, especially if she thinks it'll get her what she wants. What did she say?"

"Well, she made it sound like the engagement and the movie go hand in hand. Without one, you won't have the other. Is that true?"

"I'm making *Visions* no matter what."

"Good." With a sexy growl, she swung a leg over his lap and straddled him, wiggling against his ever-present erection.

And that was the end of it. Dropped, like it had never happened, and minus any drama. VJ might be the perfect woman. And he might have to face that his resistance to the engagement had more to do with VJ than he'd been willing to admit.

He stared into her gorgeous eyes sparking with that wealth of acceptance and understanding and suddenly couldn't speak.

Passion faded. Then all that simmering emotion had to go somewhere. What would he do then? He refused to give in to the black side of passion—the rage, the anger. The way his father did once his parents' forbidden love affair fizzled.

The right move was to disengage and shove everything back into the box. Save VJ the heartache. He never should have gotten involved with a victim of abuse. Never should have gotten involved with someone so singularly qualified to break that seal on his emotions. Maybe if they'd met later, at a point when he'd practiced balancing a whole lot more, things would be different.

Regardless, they'd met now, and he couldn't keep his hands off of her. She called to him and every cell answered, reaching out, seeking to unify at a level so deep, he hadn't realized it existed. He trusted her like he'd never trusted anyone.

If only he could trust himself as much.

As she lifted his T-shirt over his head and her soft hands sparked across his chest with sweet, intense heat, her scent drifted into the space between them, clenching his gut. He should push her away.

But he couldn't. Not yet.

He had no illusions about what VJ wanted. Expected. A happily ever after. VJ deserved that, deserved someone's whole heart forever. But what did that mean? What if he wanted to be that person but couldn't figure out how to keep his balance? Then it would be too late.

It was better to disappoint her than to take a chance.

This passion between them was going to end in a world of hurt and not all of it was going to be hers. The sooner he let her go, the sooner they could both move on.

By noon, VJ had sent Kris off to a meeting with Some Important Movie People, with strict orders to come back in a good mood, and then parked herself in front of the TV, intending to call Pamela Sue and giggle over how she'd made the news. She owed her friend some juicy details about Kris, too.

She raced through the channels to an entertainment news network. It was noon, so they'd probably lead in with more important stories. Except they were already showing pictures of her in that lovely, obscene red dress, which was currently balled up in the comforter from Kris's bed.

"…unidentified source claims Oscar-winning actress Kyla Monroe was dumped by Kristian Demetrius via phone yesterday. The source, a close friend of Ms. Monroe's, describes her as heartbroken and confused about why her longtime boyfriend would end their relationship over a women he met a few days ago."

The reporter paused as the photo of Kyla next to VJ's head morphed into one of VJ and Kris at Casa di Luigi when the sexual tension had been so high, the sparks between them were practically visible.

VJ flinched. Her fingers were in Kris's mouth in the photo—but when weren't they? She and Kris should have had more discretion. Mama would be so ashamed, especially to hear her daughter had been carrying on with a man she'd just met.

The reporter's face grew grave. "Social media is frenzied over the alleged betrayal of an actress beloved in the films *Sweet as Snow* and *Long Way Home*."

Text appeared on the screen and with a roiling stomach, VJ read the vicious slurs people had posted to various websites. Calling her a home wrecker. A boyfriend stealer, though that was ridiculous since Kyla and Kris hadn't been together. Calling her a nobody. Well, that one was true.

Who went to that much effort to say things about someone they'd never met? And over a situation they knew nothing about? Hilarious how all this was her fault. Apparently the man in a cheating and heartbreak scandal had no culpability.

Breakfast almost reappeared when the author of one of the slurs identified herself as a technician at the spa VJ had gone to. She went so far as to say she'd seen VJ's breasts and they were nothing special. As if that made it obvious Kris had chosen the wrong woman.

VJ had to get out of this room and away from the TV.

She stretched out at the pool and tried to empty her mind through sheer will. She didn't even pick up *Embrace the Rogue*. Her runaway carriage had already crashed and burned and the hero wasn't around to save her anyway.

A commotion by the pool's gate interrupted her misery. Two women in Hotel Dragonfly uniforms were blocking the pool entrance. Another woman clutching a microphone and a man with a camera tried to get past them. Even at a hundred yards, the news channel logo and the raised voices were painfully clear. It was a reporter looking for VJ.

Well, what better way to handle this than to make a statement? According to Kyla, Kris liked strong women who could take care of themselves. So she'd take care of it.

Twelve

VJ wove through the loungers and other hotel guests to the exit. "I'll talk to them," she said to the uniformed women.

"If you're sure, Ms. Lewis." The two hotel employees nodded and melted away.

The camera lens was much bigger than it had looked from the other side of the pool. The cameraman zeroed in on her bikini. She should have scheduled time later, when she was dressed. Too late now.

"I'm Rebecca Rogers from KTVN." The reporter was a sleek blonde woman in heels, with flawless makeup and a tan dark enough to draw the attention of every skin-cancer specialist in Dallas. "Ms. Lewis? Is that your name?"

"VJ Lewis. I didn't steal Kris from Kyla. Can you tell everyone?"

The reporter's expression didn't change. "Is this on the record?"

"You can quote me if that's the question. I heard what people are saying about me and it's not true. None of it is. I'm not that kind of person, who deliberately goes after a man who's unavailable."

She flinched at the lie as soon as it came out of her mouth. No, the engagement was never real and Kris wasn't actually with Kyla, but at the top of the Ferris wheel, she'd kissed a man carrying an engagement ring intended for another woman. They'd had an agreement and VJ had plunked herself down in the middle of it.

"You deny that you're intimately involved with Kristian Demetrious?" The reporter almost shoved the microphone into VJ's mouth in her eagerness.

"I'm denying that he was involved with Kyla Monroe. They weren't engaged. They're not going to be engaged. It was supposed to be a publicity stunt to promote their new movie."

That got the reporter's attention. She fired off a series of questions, and VJ answered them as best she could. She was a good girl from West Texas, not the vixen home wrecker people thought she was, and this reporter could clarify that.

"You work fast," Rebecca concluded with a smarmy grin. "This is quite a cozy arrangement you have going on with Kristian." The microphone was in her face again. The reporter asked, "What's next for you two?"

Wasn't that the million-dollar question? "That's private."

Rebecca's eyebrows rose. "But the rest of your relationship isn't?"

"It should be. But thanks to people like you, it's not. I can't sit by and let everyone believe bad things about me."

"So, you just want people to believe bad things about Kyla Monroe and Kristian Demetrious. Right? You said they were planning to pretend to be engaged as a publicity stunt."

"No." VJ shook her head and frowned. She shouldn't have said that. No one had even mentioned anything about an engagement. Except VJ. "I didn't mean for any of this to come across as bad."

"Comes with the territory. Don't shack up with celebrities

if you can't take the heat," Rebecca advised with a conde-
scending head tilt.

"This interview is over." VJ whirled and scurried to her
lounger, but the pool wasn't a sanctuary any longer. All of
this because she was chasing a happily-ever-after with Kris
that was still a happily-right-now. She snatched her bag from
the adjacent lounger and blew past Rebecca's prying eyes to
go back to the room.

By the time Kris got back from his meeting, she'd curled
up in a ball on the couch and cried all the tears her body could
produce.

He dashed into the room, tossed his phone on the coffee
table and gathered her up in his arms. "I'm sorry."

Which left no doubt he'd either seen or heard about her new-
found notoriety. This was so not what she signed up for. Casual
sex, trading off men with celebrities. Media scandals. None
of that had been on her mind when she got into the Ferrari.

"They think I'm evil," she said.

Kris's phone buzzed against the coffee table but he ignored
it.

"What can I do?" he asked softly and stroked the back of
her head.

"I don't know. None of this is your fault. I feel like the vil-
lainess in a soap opera."

The phone buzzed again.

"Answer it. Please," VJ said and jumped up. "I'll be fine.
I'm taking a shower. By myself."

His eyes tracked her as she stepped away from the couch,
but he didn't try to stop her. "Okay."

She stood under the spray for what seemed like hours and
still couldn't eliminate the oily feel to her skin. If it had been
a sleazy tabloid, *that* she could have shrugged off. Maybe. But
Rebecca the Reporter was from a local TV station and had gotten a stellar scoop by locating VJ at the Dragonfly.

When she trudged back into the main living area of the suite she slammed into the wall of Kris's mood. The atmosphere had changed like a squall line tumbling over the mountains, about to let loose a toad-strangler of a storm.

"What's wrong?" she asked.

He paced a mad trail along the carpet behind the couch, turning sharply before he hit the wall. A black band held his hair in place at his collar but it was a jumbled mess and Kris was never a mess.

"Why is your hair tied up?"

"It was irritating me." And back to pacing. "I'm trying to calm down. That's what's wrong."

Instinct told her she shouldn't press him when he was this upset, but what should she do? She couldn't sit quietly when agitation hung in the air so thick she almost needed snorkeling gear. But neither could she hide in the bedroom, away from the force of his distress on a day when so much had already gone wrong. "Is there another news story circulating about how I'm the love child of Satan and used a voodoo spell to make you break up with Kyla?"

"Not quite." He whirled and faced her, arms stiff at his sides. Unapproachable, like he'd been at the club. "There is this one circulating where you informed the media the engagement was a publicity stunt. You know. The one thing I asked you not to tell anyone."

Her eyelids flew shut, and she struggled to breathe. He *had* asked her not to say anything but she'd forgotten that.

"I'm sorry. So sorry. It slipped out. I was so upset about all the horrible things people were saying. Are you mad?"

"Mad." Wearily, he weaved to the carpet and rested his forehead on the tips of his fingers. "Mad. At you? No, I'm not."

"What are you, then?"

"One more statement to the press shy of losing my career," he said with a short laugh and it crawled across her chest with sharp needles.

Losing his *career?* Not the film and only the film? "What does that mean?"

"What it sounds like. My executive producer called, and he's a little unhappy about news coverage, which is the exact opposite of the agreed direction for *Visions of Black*'s publicity. He's threatening breach of contract. No one will work with me if that happens."

"But you're not mad?" she asked cautiously.

"I'm not happy. The engagement wasn't going to happen regardless, but I haven't had a chance to figure out an alternative. I needed that time. Kyla is beyond furious. It took me fifteen minutes to calm her down long enough to coherently explain to me what you'd done."

"That's who was calling. Before I got in the shower."

"Yeah. It should be funny. She won't admit it, but I have no doubt she's the one who told the press about you and me, trying to upset you and make you look bad. She didn't expect you to return the favor. Good job. It's rare to beat Kyla at her own game." He stared at the floor instead of at her. "I'm going to lose everything without some serious damage control. I have to go back to L.A. and start salvaging. If I'm really lucky and invest a gallon of blood, sweat and tears, I'll still be able to show my face in Hollywood."

The option where Kris ended up with her and the movie dissipated into thin air. She'd fooled herself into believing his greatest emotional need was to embrace his passionate side when in reality, he'd already embraced his passions through his career.

Film was his release, his outlet. Not her.

Even if he threw himself at her feet, vowed undying love and swore to give it all up for her—the film, his career, Hollywood, his soul, all of it—she'd tell him to get up and stop being ridiculous. That wasn't happily ever after, to gut a vibrant, brilliant man, leaving only a cavity behind. But hey, he loved her. Wasn't that all that mattered?

Not even close.

She swallowed to keep the bile down and knelt on the carpet to take his hand and squeeze it. "You can be mad at me. I deserve it. I—" Another swallow. "I screwed up, and I don't know how to fix it."

"That's not on you. I have to put my career back together. I shouldn't have even agreed to such a stupid stunt. Actually it's a relief I'll never have to do it now." Pain planted deep lines around his gorgeous mouth. "Though I wish it hadn't been ripped off the table with such final and devastating consequences."

That made two of them. "When are you leaving?"

"An hour."

"Is this it, then?"

He didn't pretend to misunderstand. "It has to be. For now. I'd like to come back and see you again, but I have no idea when. The only reason I came to Dallas is to start work on *Visions of Black*."

And there it was.

She'd also fooled herself into believing love conquered all—and that Kris sought it, too, she just had to push him into admitting it. This was a fairy tale, all right. Absolute fiction. He wasn't looking for love, not with her, or with anyone.

She wasn't special or gifted with some miraculous ability to understand him. She was nothing more than a fun diversion, which he'd been chillingly honest about.

"I understand."

"Stay in the suite as long as you want. I'll give you my number. Let me know when your condo is ready, so I can settle the bill. Don't be weird about it. Please," he said as if he'd rehearsed the lines ahead of time. Because he'd known for a while he'd be leaving, and nothing had changed except the day. "I like being your knight in shining armor charging to the rescue. That's right up your alley, isn't it?"

If only he'd said that yesterday. This morning. With a vulnerable smile as he said he loved her. At any point when she could still pretend she was woman enough to bulldoze through that wall he kept around his heart. The wall that still had a giant No Trespassing sign, despite her best efforts.

She swallowed against the hot shower of grief in her throat. "Thanks. That's very generous."

She sat frozen, staring at the wall, fighting to hold on to the belief that love could be enough to bridge the chasm between them.

"Generous," she repeated, because it was. "But I can't accept. In fact, I've already accepted too much. I'll take your address and mail you a check for everything as soon as I can."

She couldn't ask him to come back and fall in love with her when she was stable, because that dream was over, but it didn't remove her responsibility to be a strong woman who could take care of herself.

Perhaps if she had been that woman in the first place, they'd be having an entirely different conversation. He deserved someone like Kyla, a natural part of his world and an asset to his career instead of a disaster. Someone who understood him a whole lot better than she did.

"Don't go there. Please. I don't want your money. I want you to stay. I would feel better." He tilted her chin up to force her to look at him. "I'm sorry. The timing sucks. All of this sucks. I can't ask you to come to L.A. with me."

"Of course you can't. You have a reputation to recover. You can't do that with me around. I'd be in the way." She waved it off and fought back a sob. Strong women didn't fall apart when a casual relationship ended. When the man they loved didn't love them back. "You don't owe me anything. We had some fun, and I'm grateful for everything you've done. We would have parted ways eventually, right? Now's as good a time as any."

Confusion clouded his expression. "This isn't how I expected this conversation to go."

"Why? Because I fell for you a little?" She shrugged, feigning a nonchalance she could never, ever feel. He was going to lose his career over her unless she let him go, and she loved him too much to be that selfish. "Who wouldn't? This has been the most amazing fairy tale. But fairy tales aren't real. Our clock just struck midnight. I understand that, Kris. Ball's over. It's time to get back to reality."

The confusion melted from Kris's eyes and twisted the knife a little farther into her heart. He was a sucker for honesty, and she'd spoken nothing but cold hard truth. But now she had to lie to him about the most important thing.

"Reality is, I've got a bruise or two but I feel the same way when the Cowboys lose to the Redskins in overtime. I'll get over it. We've only known each other a few days."

Her voice broke. They weren't and never could be strangers.

"If that's how you feel," he said.

Maybe she *should* call Kyla's agent if he believed that. His expression was marble hard and unapproachable and she couldn't look at him anymore. "Pack, or you'll miss your plane. Check out when you leave, and I'll be right behind you."

"Where will you go?"

"Don't worry, I'll be fine. It's time I figured out how to rescue myself."

He stood and helped her up, but didn't release her hand. He hauled her into a fierce embrace, and she almost lost her flimsy grip on sanity as his familiar arms came around her, sliding her into the groove of his body no other woman could possibly fit as well. Greek whispered through her hair, and he kissed the spot where his words had branded her scalp.

"What did you say?" She pulled back and searched his expression.

"Maybe in another life." There was a glimmer in his eye, and it looked like sorrow. But it was probably only a reflection of what he saw in hers.

She fled into her room, the one she hadn't used since the

first night, and lay on the bed, hating the scratchy comforter against her raw skin. She stared at the clock with dry eyes until an hour and four minutes had passed. Then she picked up the phone on the bedside table and called Pamela Sue to wire her some money because she had no pride and no choices left.

"Thank God," Pamela Sue said when VJ identified herself. "I've been calling every hotel in Dallas for hours. Beverly Porter said you're not staying with her and no one had any idea where you went. I'm so sorry to have to tell you this, but your daddy had a heart attack."

Kris couldn't sleep. His condo was too hushed. Too cold. Too L.A. and impersonal with its mix of dark natural stone surfaces, concrete floor stained black and masculine furnishings he'd never thought twice about. It was all too…not where he wanted to be.

He plunked onto the leather sofa near the rush of a river rock waterfall in the living room and ran through scenes in his head, the same place he'd sat a thousand times. It was not working.

It was 2:00 a.m. That was pretty standard. He wore lounging pants and no shirt. Also typical. The leather chilled his back, keeping him alert and honest, and the peaceful shush of the waterfall washed street noise from the atmosphere. Totally normal.

He kept listening for VJ to tiptoe into the room, wearing that virginal white robe with the loose collar. The one so easy to slip off her soft shoulders and bare her beautiful body, allowing him access to that butterfly she'd inked—permanently—into her skin.

Not at all normal.

Why couldn't he shake her out of his system? She lingered in his mind in a persistence of memory tattooed across his consciousness. Impossible to eliminate. Impossible to embrace. He couldn't think. Couldn't eat. Couldn't feel. Never in his life had he been unable to create, to escape into the imaginary as a method to deal with reality.

That refuge was gone.

He should be storyboarding *Visions of Black,* if nothing else, but definitely working up proposals to bring in additional investors. Instead, he was obsessing over the pain and resignation on VJ's face when he'd told her he was leaving.

There'd been a moment, back in the hotel room, when he thought she was going to fall in his arms and beg him to stay. Demand that he love her like she loved him. Verbalize on his behalf what was in his heart because she saw inside him so much more clearly than he did. He'd braced for it, uncertain how he'd respond. The moment passed, and it became painfully obvious the scene wasn't going to end that way.

Instead, he'd thoroughly killed her belief in happily ever after because he couldn't find the courage to reach for it. He'd hurt her, irreparably damaging something precious.

Now he'd live in the purgatory he deserved. Recreating that scene a hundred ways but in the endings he created, he always figured out what had gone wrong before walking out the door.

He had a meeting with Jack Abrams in seven hours. In seven hours, either he'd have a plan to salvage *Visions of Black* or he'd have a front-row seat to the final demise of his career. This movie should have been the springboard, catapulting him to the next level. Not his swan song.

How had it come to this?

The intercom at the entrance to his condo buzzed, startling him out of his morose contemplation. A visitor. In the middle of the night. A short burst of hope that it might be VJ dissolved into the more likely scenario. Five bucks said it was Kyla. Blitzed.

He activated the two-way speaker, pretty sure he was going to be sorry.

"Hey, babe." The cultured feminine voice floated from the box. "In the mood for some company?"

He grimaced. At least Kyla was a happy drunk and therefore less likely to cause a scene. "No. Go home and sleep it off."

"Oh, honey, you don't have to be that way. I just want to talk. Nothing else."

Right. They hadn't spoken since her hysterical call the afternoon everything had fallen apart with VJ, but yet, here she was in L.A., itching for yet another confrontation. "Call me in the morning. It's after two."

Even so, the rush of cars and boisterous pedestrians filtered in along with Kyla's words. "Let me in. This button is hard to push, and I'm wearing five-inch heels."

"Whose fault is that?" Nothing good was going to come of this late-night visit. Nothing. "I was asleep. I'd like to go back to bed."

"Kris." She snuffled. "We were lovers for a long time. I know you weren't asleep. Unless you want a picture of me at your door on the front page of every tabloid in the morning, let me in."

That was the last thing he wanted. A conversation with Kyla was second to last. He buzzed open the lock on the entrance and dashed into the bedroom to put on a shirt. No reason to give her any further ideas since she undoubtedly had plenty of ideas already.

He opened the door and let her totter in to collapse on the couch after she'd miraculously missed tripping over the lamb's wool throw rug. Crossing his arms, he leaned on the shut door. "What's so important?"

She smoothed the microscopic lines of her fuchsia skirt and smiled demurely with flawlessly painted lips. "I wanted to see you. I miss you. Is that so bad?"

With a silent groan, he went to the kitchen and poured a glass of water. "Drink this. I'll call you a cab." He handed her the glass, and when she took it, a long wave of her perfume settled over him. The scent was cloying and sweet. He'd forgotten how much he hated its artificial quality.

"Sit down." She patted the couch and fluttered her surgically enhanced lashes. "I'm sorry about what happened in Dallas. Is your friend okay?"

He shook his head. "Not having this conversation."

Slyly, she tapped a nail on her lips and peered up at him. "Since she's not here, I assume it didn't work out. Too bad. She wasn't right for you anyway."

That explained the timing. Kyla was scoping out his residence for signs of competition.

"Who was? You?" Cursing, he went back into the kitchen so the island would be between them. Small comfort. He'd already given her far too much of an opening.

Her fake interview laugh trilled through the air. "You like to pretend things are over, but there are still feelings between us or you never would have agreed to the engagement."

He wasn't taking the bait. She could talk until laryngitis set in, and he wasn't going to let her goad him into another endless conversation about their relationship.

Except now he was thinking about it, as she'd intended.

Why had he agreed to the engagement? When the deal came together with Abrams, Kris immediately recommended Kyla for the lead role. Film was an industry, not a school yard. He couldn't let personal feelings get in the way, and after she'd read the script, her agent had contacted his assistant to say she was in.

Things had snowballed from there. His palms gripped the hard, granite edges of the island countertop, grounding him. He'd agreed—at the time—because *Visions of Black* was more important than anything else. *Was.* Now it wasn't.

"It could have been a new start for us, Kris," Kyla said and came into the kitchen. She wasn't nearly as drunk as he'd assumed. Her cornflower-blue eyes were bright and open, as if imploring him to plumb their depths and see the truth. A trick of the recessed lighting in the kitchen. Kyla never missed her mark.

She set the glass down and positioned a handful of talons on his arm. "I made a mistake. With Guy. When I told you, you got so mad. I thought that meant you cared more than you'd let on and needed space to get over it."

He could have saved her the suspense if he'd just had this conversation a long time ago instead of avoiding confrontation. "Mad because you cheated on me and lied. I never gave you one reason to treat me that way."

"That's not true." She pouted. "I was lonely, and you were so distant and focused on work. The thing with Guy happened in a moment of weakness. He was there for me."

What a cliché. "You were bored. And guess what? I don't blame you."

Improbably, he wasn't angry about Hansen. Not anymore. He had been detached and passionless with Kyla. When she'd moved on, in hindsight, he'd been relieved. He should have told her.

Kyla's confusion grew as fast as his clarity. "Does that mean you've finally forgiven me?"

"It does. Totally forgiven. You were right, there was a lack of resolution to our relationship. Thanks," he said sincerely. "For forcing the issue. I'm sorry I was so distant."

"It's okay," she said with a delicate sniff and covered his hand with hers. "I understand why you're like that. You're almost a robot. That's why you're a director, not an actor, even though you've got the look. But you stay behind the camera because you can't tap into the emotional layers necessary to be someone different in front of the camera."

Someone different? He was already someone different. The person he could only be because of VJ.

He'd disconnected from life and poured himself into his art, the only defense he thought he had against all the raging things inside. If VJ hadn't blasted his barriers apart, he'd likely have continued being a non-participant in his own story forever.

He'd tried so hard not to be his father that he'd neglected

to be Kris. Only VJ saw through his defenses, demanding his participation, forcing him into the middle of the action. Drawing him out in spite of himself.

"Is that right?" he asked.

She nodded. "You like to tell people what to do. You're a control freak, and it shuts you down inside. I can help you."

"Let me ask you something. How come we hardly ever had sex?"

A stiletto scraped against the Travertine when she half stepped, half stumbled in surprise. "You never wanted to. I assumed you had a low sex drive but were too proud to talk about it. Some macho European thing."

"How come *you* never wanted to?"

"I did. I tried. You blew me off, muttering about edits or a read-through the next day, and you'd disappear inside yourself."

That sounded about right. Excuses instead of intimacy. Justifications instead of passion. He only allowed film to excite him.

Until VJ.

"But I'm okay with that," she purred. Her hand wandered up his arm, toying with his biceps and brushing against his sleeve, as if she had every right to do so. "We'll work on it. So let's put it behind us and start over. I forgive you for that little indiscretion in Dallas and—"

He laughed and removed her hand. "You don't want to get back together. You just want something you can't have, and you can't have me. I'm in love with VJ, and I let her go like a complete idiot. I have to get her back."

Finally, *something* that made perfect, absolute sense. It was so clear now. He loved her, with ferocious terror and awe. She was his passion and had torn that lid off in her unique VJ style, unleashing a flood of emotion and creativity he had hadn't even realized was missing.

She balanced him. He'd been teetering so far in the other direction, the true danger lay in living an unengaged life, not in somehow turning violent overnight. Without VJ, his soul would shrivel back up into that person who wasn't his father, but also wasn't who he wanted to be.

Kyla's eyes widened. "She tried to destroy your career, Kris. You can't be serious."

"If my career is over, it's my fault, not hers." His career was low on the list of concerns at this moment. He'd built it from nothing once, he'd do it again. After settling more important matters. "I should've taken responsibility for the problems in my relationship with you a long time ago. If I had, the fake engagement would have died at the outset, and you wouldn't have had a chance to issue a statement about VJ. You forced her into talking to the press."

That was his mistake for ever mentioning her to Kyla, which he'd only done as yet another way to avoid his feelings. No more autopilot. VJ warranted all of his heart. All of his passion. The answer was so simple—transfer the energy he spent pretending to be something he wasn't into ensuring that the passion he felt for her never died, never changed, and was always a positive reinforcement of his love.

It might be the hardest thing he'd ever attempted. Fear hijacked his lungs, but he squeezed in a deep breath.

He'd make it happen. VJ was worth it.

"You should know better than to cross me," she said, and that was as close to an admission of guilt as he'd get. Her eyes narrowed. "She's a nobody. She'll never fit into our world."

"Then I'll put my creative energy into finding a way to fit into hers. Oh, to be clear, we're through. Finally, completely and forever. Your cab's here."

Without another word, he escorted one of the world's most beautiful and glamorous women out the door and locked it behind her. He had a lot of work to do before he could earn his happily-ever-after.

Somehow, he had to figure out a way to give VJ back the belief in it.

Thirteen

VJ hopped into Bobby Junior's ancient truck, slammed the door and stared straight ahead at the sun rising along the horizon in an inferno of heartbreaking colors. "Stop looking at me like that."

"Sorry." Her brother rested a work-roughened hand on the steering wheel. He started the truck and pulled out of Pamela Sue's driveway to make the long trek to the hospital where Daddy lay recovering. "I don't mean to."

She sighed. This was why she'd waited until this morning to ask Bobby Junior to take her to see Daddy. She'd needed a day to collect herself. A girl could only have so many illusions shattered in a week and losing the one where her oldest brother was still a hero might be the straw.

"You're dying to ask me about it. Go ahead. What do you want to know? How many times Kris and I had sex?"

Fourteen. Counting the times they'd done…other stuff. *Get over it*. She couldn't let the memories unwind or she'd blubber like a housewife watching talk shows.

"No!" Reddening, he shook his head. "I don't even want to think about that." He signaled to turn onto Little Crooked Creek Road and cleared his throat. "I have three kids. I know how they got here. It's different when it's my little sister."

"So, the lurid details are what you wanted to ask about."

It took a full five minutes before he responded. "Jamie...she wondered about the tattoo. Did you really get one?"

"You want me to come over tonight and show it to her? Show the kids?"

"VJ." Bobby Junior frowned, looking a lot like Daddy, and chomped on the ever-present gum he'd traded for chewing tobacco after the birth of his first kid. "You took off with a stranger and ran around all over Dallas, getting photographed and talked about on the news. People are curious. You ask a lot if you expect them not to be."

The folks in Little Crooked Creek could pass judgment with the best of the internet piranhas. Day before yesterday, VJ stepped off the bus and huddled on a bench to wait for Pamela Sue, only to glimpse Mrs. Pritchett caning across the street to avoid VJ. Two weeks ago, they'd shared a pew in church. VJ had held the hymnal for the eighty-year-old woman since her arthritis flared up in the August heat.

"Well, I'm sorry I caused such a ruckus trying to have a life." She laced her arms across her chest but it didn't bandage the hurt. "You can say it. I got what I deserved. I let a guy have the milk without buying the cow and then he left to go back to his real life in Hollywood. Can't expect to grow an oak tree with okra seeds, right?"

Kris's business card was burning a hole in her pocket. He'd written his cell-phone number on the back in swirly numerals and left it on the coffee table of their—his—hotel room. No message, no indication of why. He'd probably left it accidentally. With no intention of pulling it out until she could write him a check, she'd tucked it into her bag. As a memento of what happened in real life when she forgot that fairy tales were for books.

"That's not what I was going to say." His back stiffened, pulling away from the cracked bench seat. "Daddy was bad after you left. Worse than normal. Went off on a tear, throwing furniture around. Mrs. Johnson called the sheriff when he drove through her flowerbed at midnight. I had to pick him up, still drunk, from the clink."

Bobby Junior's quiet condemnation dug into her stomach with claws. She'd walked out on her responsibilities. Lots of people had to deal with parents and life and real hardships. They didn't leave. "I guess that's my fault, too, same as the heart attack."

"Daddy's heart attack wasn't your fault. Yeah, he got a shock seeing you on TV and hearing the things people were saying. But the doctor said it was the stress of Mama and a year of hard drinking. I would have told you that if you'd come around instead of hiding out at Pamela Sue's."

"I'm here now. I'm being a good daughter and going to see Daddy, aren't I?"

Wounds from the night she left Little Crooked Creek were still fresh and coupled with the new ones, she couldn't have done this any sooner. All of yesterday had been spent in the fetal position on Pamela Sue's bed, alternately bawling and staring at the wall.

Then Daddy had taken a turn for the worse, and she'd forced herself to push back the grief. What if he died before she saw him again? She didn't want to have to live with that. He was still her father.

The shoulder where she'd stopped to check out the sleek Ferrari flew by in a flash. Just like her relationship with Kris. Relationship—or whatever it was called when a person blinks and the highlight of her existence vanishes, leaving only a sharp memory too vivid to erase and too painful to enjoy.

She'd only meant to drool over the car. Not the driver. Or

his hands. His mouth. The way he opened up when he was inside her and his soul spoke without any words. And when he did talk...her eyelids fluttered closed and time stopped while she ached.

She missed Kris, and it was a slow, agonizing death instead of the difficult, but eventual, recovery she'd hoped for.

Bobby Junior took a deep breath, jerking her out of her misery. "Why didn't you tell me what Daddy did to you?"

"Which part?" she asked, too surprised he'd found out to answer right away.

His hands were clamped so tight on the steering wheel, veins popped. "When I picked up Daddy from the sheriff, he was babbling about how he'd driven you away. I finally got him to tell me he'd taken all your money." Bobby Junior paused for a beat. "And that he hit you."

She shrugged. "What difference would it have made if I had told you?"

"What difference—" He thumped the seat between them, startling her with the force. "You could have stayed with me and Jamie. Let us help you get your money back. You're so independent. There's nothing wrong with asking for a little help. Why didn't you?"

Her throat hurt from the twinge in Bobby Junior's voice. How selfish she'd been to leave without thinking how others might take it. She probably should have told her brothers about Daddy hitting her, too, but she'd been so sure no one would take her side. "I don't know."

"I do. You're just like Mama. Both of you take charge. The whole time Mama was sick, you did what had to be done. I don't know where you found that grit. Then she—" His voice broke and he swallowed. "She died and all of us were lost. Except you. You took care of the funeral. Daddy. The boys. Everyone except yourself. I'm surprised it took so long for you to break. Woulda been nice if your rebellion had been a little safer and lower profile."

"Pamela Sue made me promise to use condoms." Which wasn't everything she wanted to say but her throat closed.

The blush, not quite gone anyway, flared up and spread from his cheeks to his neck. "Glad to hear it," he said gruffly and tapped her chest. "But I meant safer in here. You're different. Your shoulders are heavier."

"I grew up. It was past time. I have to face reality, not live in a fantasy world where an exciting man sweeps me off my feet, only to disappear at midnight."

All of a sudden, it didn't seem so devastating to be back in Little Crooked Creek, still broke, but not in such a bad place after all. Some maids became princesses, and some women just became self-sufficient. When she'd left the first time, options were hard to come by and the one promising excitement and escape won. Now, because of Kris, she had the wisdom to evaluate opportunity openly, honestly and without a coating of fairy dust. That's what strong women did. Like Mama. Like her.

"Want me to kick his butt? I'd like to think you still need me for something." Her brother's affable gap-toothed grin settled her heart. Not completely, but along with the gift of absolution, it went a long way. He ruffled her hair like he had for as long as she could remember.

She smiled at her brother and patted his arm. "Thanks. That means a lot."

Downtown Van Horn unrolled through the windshield as Bobby Junior drove down the main street lined with adobe-plastered stores, family-owned Mexican restaurants and dust. West Texas still wasn't for her. She'd find a way to get back to Dallas and start building a life on her own terms. A life based in reality.

He pulled into the hospital lot and parked, then threw an arm around her shoulders to walk with her into the lobby. They sat by Daddy's bedside for a few hours, talking to each other, talking to Daddy without expectation of a response, smiling at the nurses. Daddy woke up once and squeezed VJ's hand. It was enough. She'd find a way to forgive him. Not today, but eventually. Some hurts went too deep to heal easily.

When the truck pulled into Pamela Sue's driveway, her friend sprinted out and opened the door. She pushed VJ to the center, then bounced onto the vacated seat. "What took you so long?" she asked, breathlessly. "We have to go down to Pearl's. Drive, Bobby."

"What's at Pearl's?" he asked, as he shifted into Reverse and peered at the rearview mirror. "I got to get back to the garage."

"It's a surprise for VJ," she said. "Drop us off and ske-daddle."

VJ gave Pamela Sue a one-eyed stare. "A surprise like pin a scarlet letter on VJ or more like a surprise public flogging of VJ?"

When Pamela Sue had picked her up from the bus station, VJ'd asked to visit Pearl first, to apologize for leaving her former boss in the lurch. Pearl was a marshmallow, so she wouldn't be the one pinning or flogging, but as for the rest of the town, it was anyone's guess.

"Neither. Wait and see." In a very un–Pamela Sue way, she kept her mouth closed clear through the single stoplight in the center of town. Right before Bobby Junior turned the corner at Pearl's, she asked, "Are you sure you don't want to come in, Bobby? You might be sorry you missed it."

Now VJ was really curious. Oh. Everyone had missed her birthday. Surprise party, of course. She whimpered. Normally, she'd love that but with folks' dirty looks and general hostility, attendance would be slim.

But then she caught sight of the parking lot at Pearl's. It was full. Jam-packed, with cars and trucks lining the street for a block, and people streaming through the front doors.

Eyes wide, she glanced at Pamela Sue. "It *is* a public flogging. I'm suddenly feeling very feverish."

"Just get out." She hooked elbows with VJ and hauled her

out of the truck the second Bobby Junior braked at the curb. The engine shut off, and Bobby Junior swung out of the cab.

"Can't stay but a minute," he said in concession.

All three of them trooped inside. The diner was dark—the kitchen, the dining room, entrance—but the rustle of people was unmistakable. The lights flashed and everyone yelled, "Surprise!" but there were no decorations, no cake and no balloons.

Instead, a line of people stood in the middle of the room, each holding a single yellow sunflower. Confused and a little weirded out, she turned to Pamela Sue. "What is this?"

"Take the flowers," she said, which was no answer at all, and dragged her toward Mrs. Johnson, who was at the head of the line. VJ trailed after Pamela Sue, only because their arms were still hooked.

Mrs. Johnson extended the flower, which had a rectangle of white attached to it with a silky ribbon, and said, "I liked the red dress."

A compliment. Not a judgmental put-down. Mystified, VJ gripped the sunflower, held it to her nose and inhaled the fresh fragrance. The dress hung in the back of the closet at Pamela Sue's. Another memento she couldn't toss. "Thanks. I liked it, too."

"Read the card," someone in the audience urged.

Intrigued, she flipped the card and took in the words. Her stomach seized up like an overheated engine. The card shook so hard in her trembling fingers, it was a wonder she held on to it. "I can't. It's Greek. I don't know how to translate it."

"I do," Kris said from behind her.

She spun and oh, *yes*. There he was, in the flesh. Clad in black, ebony hair falling against his cheekbones, arms crossed and one hip leaned gracefully against the discolored wall. Beautifully, sinfully gorgeous and—

Dear Lord. Every person in this room knew they'd been

intimate. Frozen, she stared at him. Couldn't move, couldn't breathe. One hand flew up to cover her mouth.

Kris straightened and strode toward her, eyes fluid and searching and beguiling. He stopped a couple feet away but didn't touch her.

His phone buzzed.

The only thing she could think to say was, "You went to the communication dark side and started carrying your phone in your pocket?"

With a wry laugh that almost broke the tension, he pulled it out and pitched the phone at the closest table. "I kept hoping you might call, and I didn't want it to go to voice mail."

She was the person too important to leave a message?

"What are you doing here?"

All around them, fascinated faces watched her and Kris, blurring into a ménage of colors as it crystallized.

He was here. In Little Crooked Creek.

"I'm doing what I should have done in Dallas when you said it was time to get back to reality." He edged closer, his sensual aura overwhelming. "My reality isn't the same anymore. You destroyed it and gave me something better. A reality where fairy tales come true. I'm here to recapture that reality."

His voice washed over her, flowing through the coldness inside, heating her thoroughly. She must be asleep. Dreaming. Tentatively, she reached out and flattened a palm against Kris's chest. Solid. Warm. Amazing. Real. It took every ounce of will not to sink into his arms.

This was all wrong.

"Kris." She shook her head and snatched her arm back. "You don't want that. You never wanted anything other than to make movies, and I ruined that."

The taut lines around his sculpted mouth softened. "You're wrong. I was wandering around in the desert, lost, and didn't even realize it until you found me. You showed me how to tap into my emotions. To tell the story from my heart. Without you, my career is nothing. I'd abandon it in a second if that would prove it to you."

"No! I can't let you do that," she said fiercely and took a step back. He was too close, and her will was only so strong. "You shouldn't even be here. Go back to Hollywood and get photographed a bunch with Kyla so people forget about me. Then maybe you can still make *Visions of Black*."

"You're the only person I want to be photographed with." A camera, a huge professional number like from a movie set, appeared in his hands from its hiding place under a table. He pushed some buttons and positioned it carefully on the scarred Formica tabletop. Suddenly, the camera was on them both, recording.

Kris took her hand and squeezed, so she couldn't move out of range. "This time, everyone, especially the media, will get the story right. Once upon a time, there was this guy who had all these chaotic, extreme emotions inside, and he was so afraid of letting those things control him, he pretended he didn't feel anything at all. Then he met this extraordinary woman who really got that. And this guy fell in love with her but couldn't figure out how to get past being that same guy so he let her go. Now he's trying to get her back."

Kris was in love with her? Definitely a dream. "How does the story end?"

"With a translation." He nodded to the card hanging from the sunflower still clutched in her fist. "It says, 'The first time I saw you, you reminded me of a living sunflower. Beautiful and open.'"

With a firm hand, he guided her to the next person, who held the next flower. Her third-grade teacher, Mrs. Cole, smiled and handed off the bloom. "I'm jealous you got to stay in such a fancy hotel," she said with a wink.

Coupled with Mrs. Johnson's nice comment, it warmed her. Not everyone thought she was the devil incarnate. These people were here to support her. They were here because Kris had asked them to be. He was rescuing her from the bad press, because that was what he did.

Kris leaned in, brushing her ear with his lips and as her lobe burned, he said, "This one reads, 'The second time I saw you, your hair smelled like coconut, and I couldn't get the scent out of my mind.'"

Where was he going with all this loveliness? Before she could blink, Kris shuttled her to the next flower, held by Pearl. "This card says, 'I nicknamed you my desert mirage, a shimmering, gorgeous fantasy rising up out of the bleak landscape.'"

A nickname. *Oh, no.* "The stages. You have all the stages written down on these cards."

Impishly, Kris smiled and handed her another flower. "'The Scrambler. Then the Ferris wheel.'"

He was reading the cards in public. Great balls of fire. *In public.*

"Everybody out. Now." She turned to address the room at large before Kris could start on the next flower, which undoubtedly read: *You exposed your breast, showed me the butterfly tattoo and I tasted it in the elevator.* "I appreciate everyone coming out today. Your support means a lot. But some things are best done without an audience."

Grumbling, everyone shuffled to their feet and filed out slower than lizards molt. The flower bearers laid the stalks in a pile on a nearby table. Pamela Sue grinned and hustled a glowering Bobby Junior out the door. VJ made a mental note to thank her later for taking care of all this.

Finally, they were alone.

Alone, with Kris. She never thought she'd see him again, never mind while he spouted romanticisms in that gorgeous voice.

"I wasn't going to read them all aloud," he said. "That's why I wrote them in Greek."

"What else do the cards say?" she asked, her throat raw with emotions too big to process.

"Lots of things. Like, how I love being your guinea pig. Six-forty-five, which is what time I watched the sunrise while I held you. This one." He pulled a bloom from the stack and swept it across her cheek. "This one says, 'Love, passion and friendship. You gifted me with all three, and I want to spend my life giving them back to you.'"

He dropped the flower, pulled something out of his back pocket and held it up. Her lungs collapsed.

A ring box.

Hesitantly, he fingered a lock of her hair. "I didn't put it in a big box and let you unwrap it. Our relationship is based on honesty. I didn't want you to have to guess. So you know right up front that I'm asking you to marry me."

"Why?" she blurted out because her brain was stuck. Her pulse was stuck. Everything was stunned into immobilization.

His stormy eyes roamed over her face. "There's only one reason to marry someone, or so you've thoroughly convinced me. Because I love you and can't live without you."

God Almighty. Kris had been possessed by aliens. "Eh." She waved it off. "You're only suffering from a hormonal imbalance."

Without missing a beat, he flipped the hinged lid and took the ring, holding it out between two steady, golden fingers. "It's inscribed. Will you read it?"

Gingerly, she accepted the pale circle of metal—Holy Heaven, it was a huge, beautiful square-cut diamond exploding with fire—and read the inscription carved into the platinum. Her knees turned to jelly.

Stage Seven is Forever.

When she couldn't speak, he said, "At Casa di Luigi, you told me I'd hit all the stages. But I missed one. Happily ever after." He plucked the ring from her fingertips. "Will you allow me to put this on?"

This wasn't solely a rescue, some elaborate scheme he'd invented to save her reputation. He was balancing the scales, legitimizing their relationship. Transforming her with his magic-wand-engagement-ring into Mrs. Demetrious.

"You're crazier than a drunk June bug." Or she was. She hardly knew which way was up. Was this some kind of setup? A different approach to publicity? "What's happening with *Visions of Black?*"

"It's a mess, but I don't care. Resolving it is meaningless unless I fix us first. I can't function without you. I can't think, can't concentrate. I need you more than I need to breathe. Please."

He was truly hurting. The evidence was there, in his rigid stance and the pain in his tumultuous expression. Hurting, because he was in love with her, like head-over-heels, Romeo and Juliet, take-a-bullet-for-her in love. Refusing him might result in as much of a gutting as his lost career. What was she supposed to do?

Once, when she was still blinded by stupidity and had an overinflated sense of her ability to read this profound man, she'd have known what to say, how to act. He'd destroyed that in Dallas, and she didn't know how to get it back.

"VJ, I messed up by not grabbing what we had." Clearly disconcerted, he exhaled and shoved his free hand through his hair. "But I'm not afraid anymore. I'm on this side of the camera, in the middle of the scene with you, exactly where I want to be. Begging you to believe in me, to believe in happily ever after again after I broke your heart. What can I say to convince you I'm sincere?"

"That was a pretty good start," she mumbled, her heart too busy duking it out with her brain to come up with a better response. "You can't marry me. We've known each other barely a week."

He cupped her chin, lifted it. The touch of his fingertips on her face almost split her in two.

"The length of our acquaintance is irrelevant, *agapi mou,*" he said, drawing her into his melty-brown eyes. "There's been something between us from the first. You feel it, too. You knew immediately you didn't want to marry that other guy. Why can't I be certain in an instant that you're the one?"

Where had this stuff *come* from? He'd blown far past romance instruction, *far* past any romance novel, into territory she'd never dreamed existed. With no experience and no clues, she didn't trust herself, didn't believe she could ever fathom the mind of Kristian Demetrious. What if she was wrong? What if it wasn't real love? What if—

In a flash, the answer came to her. With the smallest bit of dawning hope, she asked, "What kind of car do you have? At home?"

"What? A BMW SUV. So I can haul around equipment."

German. Still foreign and complex and incomprehensible.

"And a '67 Mustang," he continued as an afterthought. "I only drive it occasionally. It's the quintessential American car, symbolic of my U.S. citizenship. What does this have to do with anything?"

A Ford. Kris had a Ford in his garage.

"With a 428 V-8 engine?"

When he nodded, tears finally burst the dam and flowed down her cheeks. It was the first engine she'd ever touched, the one she'd learned everything from. She could take the entire thing apart and rebuild it. One-handed.

The coincidence didn't mean anything. Not really, but it broke her resistance. Her greatest emotional need was the heart of this man, and he was spilling it out, passionately, with soul-wrenching truth. Offering her something real, tied up with a fairy-tale bow, and asking if she was woman enough to accept.

"And you're crying because?" he asked.

"Because I love you. Put the ring on, Kristian."

The storm clouds finally cleared from his eyes as he slid the circle of forever onto her finger. Then he kissed her. It was joyous, magical, right.

Almost.

She pulled back. "Um, can you turn off the camera? I'm about four seconds from stripping you, and a sex-tape scandal might not be the best move for us."

His rich laughter took up residence in her heart, and she believed again. Not in a fantasy, but in real, true love.

Epilogue

Kris tossed the phone onto the island in the middle of his kitchen. *No way* had that just happened. He barged into the master bathroom, raring for a confrontation, anticipating it, because he never had to pretend he was emotionless ever again.

Coconut-scented bubble bath hit him at the threshold and ignited that primal reaction that hadn't faded. At all. His mind drained of everything except for the scene before him. VJ soaked in the tub, spread out appetizingly, with her eyes closed, hair wet and pure bliss in her smile. The diamond on her third finger caught the light and refracted, splintering through his heart.

She'd moved into his condo only a month ago, sliding into it as if she'd always been there. Her presence alone lightened the darkness of the decor as if he had a private sun all his own. Only a month, and already the preproduction work on *Visions of Black* was done. Brilliantly, and largely due to VJ, his stellar new production assistant.

Love was the greatest muse of all. How had he ever created without her? How had he ever lived?

She popped an eye open and regarded him steadily, shamelessly naked and gorgeous.

"Are you going to watch or get in?" she asked, her voice husky. "If it's the former, I should move some of these bubbles."

In a slow, sensuous scrape, she swished them from her breasts and the red butterfly peeped up from the foam. That butterfly—the color of passion and permanent. Every waking moment, he labored to live up to what it represented. To be worthy of the faith she'd had in him from the beginning.

Familiar quickening spiked through his groin, but he crossed his arms instead of flinging clothes to the floor. "I'm not falling for that again. Figure out a different way to distract me because—" With a sigh, he turned his back to the provocative sight of his soon-to-be-wife. "Never mind. It still works."

VJ laughed. "What am I trying to distract you from this time?"

"Kyla called. A warning might have been nice." He tried to sound stern and failed. "She was letting me know, oh-so-casually, how excited she was to start shooting since you talked her into taking a percentage of profits instead of the upfront fee her contract called for."

What a relief. A huge, gigantic relief to have that albatross off his shoulders. The film was all downhill from here.

"What? I'm not allowed to rescue you occasionally? Too bad if you don't like it. That's stage eight, by the way, and I'm bound to think of a few more," she said with a little splash, as if she'd risen from the water, perhaps exposing the butterfly fully. "Wedding's in three days. Last chance to back out."

"No way, *agapi mou.*" He twisted and ripped off his T-shirt, followed swiftly by the rest of his clothes. He stepped down, sank into the water filling the enormous garden tub and spooned VJ into his arms. Definitely his favorite position. "You're stuck with me. I gave up half my bed for you, after all."

"It's only fair. I gave up a half of a condo in Dallas for you. Though I have a feeling Beverly Porter and Pamela Sue are going to kill each other before too much longer," she said drily and settled back into that place only she fit. Wet cinnamon hair splayed across his chest, warming his skin and his heart.

Now. He had to join with this amazing woman who had saved him, and within seconds, it was a reality. The best reality because it was a combination of passion, love, friendship and a touch of magic.

Happily ever after had a lot to recommend it.

Six months passed in a blur of pleasure. Kris married VJ in a fairy-tale wedding and took her on a two-week honeymoon to Fiji, which was as far out of the state of Texas as he could get. He fell more in love with his wife every day.

He filmed *Visions of Black* on a shoe-string budget like in the old days, and discovered an interesting secret. Turned out when he put his heart into directing, cast and crew alike responded with vivid performances. The media, never hesitant to jump on a good story, devoted a great deal of coverage to the romance between the director and the woman who inspired him.

During the whirlwind of positive publicity following a surprise record-breaking opening weekend for *Visions of Black,* a reporter asked Kris how he knew it was true love with VJ. With a laugh, he said, "She told me, step by step, the secrets of romance. And she keeps telling me every day. Fortunately, I pay attention to the things she says."

* * * * *

USA TODAY Bestselling Author

Catherine Mann

presents

PLAYING FOR KEEPS

Available April 2013 from Harlequin® Desire!

Midway through the junior high choir's rehearsal of "It's a Small World," Celia Patel found out just how small the world could shrink.

She dodged as half the singers—the female half—sprinted down the stands, squealing in fan-girl glee. All their preteen energy was focused on racing to where he stood.

Malcolm Douglas.

Seven-time Grammy Award winner.

Platinum-selling soft rock star.

And the man who'd broken Celia's heart when they were both sixteen years old.

Malcolm raised a stalling hand to his ominous bodyguards while keeping his eyes locked on Celia, smiling that million-watt grin. Tall and honed, he still had a hometown-boy-handsome appeal. He'd merely matured—now polished with confidence and whipcord muscle.

She wanted him gone.

For her sanity's sake, she *needed* him gone. But now that he was here, she couldn't look away.

He wore his khakis and Ferragamo loafers with the easy confidence of a man comfortable in his skin. Sleeves rolled up on his chambray shirt exposed strong, tanned forearms and musician's hands.

Best not to think about his talented, nimble hands.

His sandy-brown hair was as thick as she remembered. It was still a little long, skimming over his forehead in a way that once called to her fingers to stroke it back. And those blue eyes—heaven help her…

There was no denying, he was all man now.

What in the hell was he doing here?

Malcolm hadn't set foot in Azalea, Mississippi, since a judge crony of her father's had offered Malcolm the choice of juvie or military reform school nearly eighteen years ago. Since he'd left her behind—scared, *pregnant* and determined to salvage her life.

But they weren't sixteen anymore, and she'd put aside reckless dreams the day she'd handed her newborn daughter over to a couple who could give the precious child everything Celia and Malcolm couldn't.

She threw back her shoulders and started across the gym.

She refused to let Malcolm's appearance yank the rug out from under her blessedly routine existence. She refused to give him the power to send her pulse racing.

She refused to let Malcolm Douglas threaten the future she'd built for herself.

What is Malcolm doing back in town?

Find out in

PLAYING FOR KEEPS

Available April 2013 from Harlequin® Desire!